Gateway of the Sun

An unforgettable story
immersed in the culture and
conflict of the Inca Empire.

Lori Wagner

Gateway of the Sun
Copyright © 2008 by Lori Wagner
Illustrated by Noelle Wagner-Kalajian

ISBN 978-0-9798627-2-4
Library of Congress Control Number: 2007907040

Requests for information should be addressed to:
Affirming Faith
1181 Whispering Knoll Lane
Rochester Hills, MI 48306
loriwagner@affirmingfaith.com
www.affirmingfaith.com

Cover design by Glenn Hall
www.glennhallphotography.com

Printed in the United States of America.

DEDICATION

This book is dedicated to students of all ages interested in looking beyond today's textbooks for a more encompassing view of political, cultural and religious history.

Specifically, I dedicate *Gateway of the Sun* to Noelle, Charles, Hope and Ashley with a prayer that, as Huallpa chooses, they also will choose to look for the good, even in difficult situations.

TEACHERS PRAISE
GATEWAY OF THE SUN

The poignant story of an orphaned boy and his sister, *Gateway of the Sun* delivers a wealth of information about the customs and beliefs practiced during the Incan reign. Author Lori Wagner provides a unique glimpse into the demise of the empire and the transition of its people from paganism to monotheism in this sometimes excruciating coming-of-age story. More than the tale of the young protagonist, Huallpa, this book also chronicles the metamorphosis of the society and culture in which he lives. As a former teacher, I highly recommend *Gateway of the Sun* for upper middle school readers and above. In addition to the extensive list of resource materials, the discussion questions and glossary of Quechuan words make this book an excellent choice for individuals or classroom use.

~ *Gretchen O'Donnell*
Rochester Hills, MI

Having taught elementary children for 30 years, I have come across many wonderful books that I have shared with my classes. *Gateway of the Sun,* without exception, is one of those books I would like to share. I was totally taken in by the author's depiction of Peru's beautiful countryside, its people, and religious rituals. I found myself being pulled into the story when Huallpa, a young man of thirteen, had the responsibility of raising his younger sister after his parents' death. Young people, as well as adults, will find the book intriguing, as they follow Huallpa's journey through the Peruvian jungle. After reading Lori Wagner's first book, I had great expectations for another. I was not disappointed and neither will you be when you read *Gateway of the Sun.*

~ *Barbara Barton*
Clarkston, MI

CONTENTS

ACKNOWLEDGMENTS

Thank you once again, my dear family, for your continued support of my writing and speaking endeavors—especially my husband Bill who has the "honor" of hearing my stories first . . . and second . . . and third, depending on the number of rewrites.

Speaking of rewrites, a big thank you (properly punctuated and in perfect subject-verb agreement) goes to Dorene Lilley with much appreciation for your editing and proofreading skills. Thanks also to Barbara Barton, Evans Bissonette, Gretchen O'Donnell and Roger Marshall for your time evaluating the manuscript.

Thank you, Bilingual Press and author John Curl for permission to include the English interpretation of ancient Inca poetry in Chapter 2.

If thanks can extend into the heavens, I offer them to my deceased husband, Peter Kalajian, for taking me to Peru on our honeymoon. It was an adventure I will never forget that planted a love for the magnificent country and its people in my heart.

And, of course, I thank the Lord for giving me breath, the ability to string words together in sentences, and the story line for *Gateway of the Sun*.

FOREWORD

Readers of *Gateway of the Sun* may find the unfamiliar customs and experiences of the Inca people hard to believe; however, careful research uncovered the obscure details brought to light in this story.

Established in 1438 A.D., the Inca reign lasted fewer than 100 years. At its height, the empire stretched from Ecuador to northern Chile and included over ten million people. Five centuries after the invasion of the Spanish in 1532 A.D., the customs and architectural achievements of the Inca Indians continue to intrigue people around the world.

Soldiers and monks documented religious and cultural practices, struggles for political power and battles with devastating disease. In addition to written history, architectural ruins, skeletons and mummified remains testify of events played out long ago in the mysterious Andes Mountains.

As you journey with Huallpa on his path to the Gateway of the Sun, consider that his story, though fiction, could relate the experiences of a real 13-year old Quechuan boy.

PROLOGUE

Just one more. I pushed through my fatigue and lifted a complaining thigh over the final stone riser. Thankful to be on level ground after the rigorous climb, I crossed the granite threshold and stood once more on the circular grass floor of the Gateway of the Sun. The steep path had challenged my body more than I expected, and a sigh slipped out as I leaned back, head and shoulders against a curved wall.

For long minutes I stood drinking thin mountain air, awaiting the return of my pulse's normal rhythm. Cold from the stonework seeped through my tunic cooling my skin, refreshing me from the effort of the climb and the sun's assault. With a pinch, the damp fabric of my tunic released its hold on my chest, and I set my gaze on the scene spread out before me.

It's as magnificent as I remembered.

Large openings between the granite stone columns of the Gateway's roofless structure framed extraordinary displays of nature and the human artistry of the barren mystical city below. Vast colors splashed the landscape—the sky a blue so crisp I could almost hear it crackle as it dashed against the brilliant green mountains rising and falling in jagged wonder across the face of the land.

In contrast to the rough terrain, fluffs of cloud skittered about the sky to silent music, propelled by breezes that brushed my face and arms. My thoughts drifted, riding the wings of a condor flying below me.

The sound of men approaching invaded the quiet. Through one of the openings, I saw a group of porters hurrying up

5

the winding trail in my direction. Within moments the band of ragged men packing colorful woven bundles burst through the passage in single file. Well formed muscles bulged beneath the weight of their burdens as they jogged through the Gateway then slipped wordlessly through the opening on the other side.

The sudden appearance of another porter startled me. He was a unique little man with graying hair that shot out like straw from beneath his worn cap. A wrinkled, sun-darkened face told me his story — one of hard work and exposure so common among our people.

Our eyes met, and the old man tipped his head in greeting. Charcoal eyes sparkled in wrinkled beds, and as he drew near, broken teeth flashed in a widening smile.

With boyish delight, he lifted his hand to show me his prize — a dead snake dangling from a string. I acknowledged his trophy with a grin and nod of my own, then the little man continued his journey, still beaming his snaggle-toothed pleasure, still holding up the scaly reptile bobbing up and down with each step.

He went the way of his fellow travelers, disappearing through the opening on the opposite side of the summit to the cities far below. The sound of swift steps fell away.

Alone again my mind raced . . .
    backwards in time . . .
        rushing down the Inca Trail before these men
            to days gone by, to another snake encounter on the same mountain path many years past.

It was my first journey to this place, and the snake I confronted that day had been very much alive.

I willed the disturbing thoughts from my mind, and chose to think instead on earlier days—happy times of boyhood spent with family before stepping foot on the path that changed my life forever.

Chapter 1

Huallpa
The Son of Joy

An involuntary jerk roused me from a fitful sleep. Trembling in the darkness, I bolted upright on my mat and fought the fear threatening to overtake me. With a shaky hand, I wiped a bead of sweat from my brow.

Not yet adjusted to the dim light, my eyes squinted out nervous glances that darted about the room counting the lumps on the floor. One. Two and three. The cradle wobbled as the baby turned in her sleep—that makes four.

Relief broke through my runaway emotions, and with each breath, the engulfing dread ebbed from my spirit.

They are here.

I am not alone.

I shook my head, hoping to dispel the lingering images, and resolved to forget the terrible dream. After all, my life and family are secure, unlike the chilling visions that stalk me in the land of sleep. The dark scenes repeated these last nights are not real. My family members sleep peacefully beside me safe in our home.

I slid back down upon my mat, tucked a woolen blanket around my shoulders and closed my eyes.

Please let me sleep again.

Summer is still here. Golden stalks of maize tickle the azure sky with fuzzy fingers. Knotted pumpkin vines heavy with orange-yellow fruit twist about on terraced gardens while abundant treasure hides beneath potato plants rooted in the earth's fragrant, rich soil. Lord Sun's nourishing rays beam upon our little village nestled between the Urubamba Valley and the city of Cuzco.

My family weaves, even Father and my uncles, which is uncommon among our people. Usually women make textiles, but we toil together in our clan called ayllu, working our trade and sharing with our relatives.

Mother is always busy. Like most people of our class, her hands constantly hold a project, though I think it would be nice if they sometimes held Pisco, my baby sister. But that is not the Runa way.

Rich or poor, Runa mothers bestow as little care possible upon their children. I remember Pisco wailed desperately inside our stone house after her birth. When I asked Father if she was well, he said Mother bathed her in cold water—that mothers accustom their babies early in life for cold temperatures, unselfishness, and hard work.

Pisco spent her first three months, day and night, swaddled in her cradle, a four-footed bench with one leg shortened. The uneven tilt caused the cradle to rock as she wriggled inside on a hammock made of thick netting, the same netting that wrapped around the sides to keep her from falling out.

Three times a day, morning, noon and night, Mother broke away from weaving or household duties, leaned over Pisco's cradle and allowed the baby to nurse. This is the people's way, feeding babies only at certain times, like other animals with their young. To hold the baby and give her milk every time she cried would make her want to suck all day, and she would become dirty with vomitings. Besides, Mother did not want to raise a great eater.

Pisco cried when she was young, but she is growing and learning to be a good Runa baby. At seven months old, her arms are no longer bound in strips of cloth, and she is able to leave her cradle during the day. Father dug a hole in the ground for her in the common area where we gather to work. Wrapped in napkins, Pisco entertains herself jumping and kicking in the hole, playing with a wooden spoon.

"Come, Pisco," said Mother. She lifted the baby from the hole. "It is time for you to eat."

Mother sat on the ground for the feeding. Kneeling at her side, Pisco steadied herself with her small hands as she nursed. When she finished at one breast, she crept around Mother to drink from the second. In this way, she was not held beyond what was necessary as she drank or changed position.

"Pisco is a noisy eater," Father said as the little one completed her meal.

"Yes," said Mother. She deposited the satisfied child in her hole and adjusted clean napkins around her bare legs. "All your children eat heartily, Husband," she said with a twinkle in her dark eyes.

Mother rose and smoothed her dress. She picked up a gourd and gave it a shake that sent the dried seeds inside dancing. Delighted by the sound, Pisco grabbed the hard-shelled fruit with tiny fingers and immediately stuck it in her mouth. The rattling continued as Pisco bounced and drool ran over the gourd.

Finished tending the baby, Mother joined the rest of the family seated in the common area. Baskets of weaving materials and tools at our sides, we worked and chatted in the grassy clearing wreathed with stone homes.

"Huallpa," Mother called, "are you ready to begin, Son?"

"I think so," I replied, carefully unwinding spun llama fibres from a wooden spindle.

My hands have grasped spindles and yarn from an early age. Since my cousins and I bounced in the pits beside our mothers, we played with the tools and studied the craft of weaving. Through the years, we continued watching and eventually began working the fibres ourselves. Without instruction we learned, and at seven I made my first narrow weaving called a jakima.

To make the jakima ribbon, I wound threads around two stakes in the ground then cut them into equal strands. I fashioned the threads into a framework, and then the fun began—shuttling colorful yarns back and forth, creating my own village pattern of which I was so familiar.

That was a memorable day, and today is special, too. I begin weaving my own manta.

Mantas are important textiles. Every family member uses and appreciates them. Made of two woven sections stitched together, mantas are used to carry things — like babies, fruits and vegetables, and firewood. We sit on them as we work, and spread them out for visitors to show hospitality.

Each village creates its own unique pattern and coloring, so mantas identify our communities like banners or flags. This afternoon, with family gathered around, I am excited to begin weaving a manta of my own.

I measured lengths of thread to make the loom for the first half and listened with interest as the conversation shifted to the upcoming festival. We are in the ninth moon, and people will soon gather from across the land to participate in religious purification ceremonies. Because it marks the beginning of the rainy season, which often brings much sickness, we celebrate the feast of Situa at this time. Offering prayers and sacrifices to Creator God, we ask Him to shield us from sickness and death.

Father knelt, crushing red nuchu blossoms to dye the wool beside him. "The chief council and lords gather at the golden temple today," he said. "They meet with Huayna Capac and the High Priest to plan the purification festival."

"The temple must be glorious today," Mother said peeking from beneath her cap. She paused the flight of her shuttle through the loom and lifted her face to receive the sun's caress upon her flat bronze cheeks.

Today Lord Sun shines upon my village and must surely visit his temple, Qoricancha, inside the city boundaries. As the adults continued discussing the upcoming festivities, I gave way to my imaginations and thought of the holy place.

No building rivals the golden splendor of Qoricancha. Massive cut granite stones set together in thin layers of silver make up the temple walls. More than seven hundred sheets of gold cover the walls decorated with intricate carvings and studded with emeralds and other gemstones in brilliant groupings. The surrounding golden courtyard contains life-sized sculptures of llamas, babies, and a field of maize all fashioned from pure gold. Even the floors are covered in gold.

Facing eastward, in the opening of the temple, a great golden likeness of his own heavenly body greets Lord Sun each morning. The face of the idol, detailed in precious stones, is surrounded by golden rays that send forth blessings from the sacred orb.

Lord Sun reigns beneath Creator God, the One invisible God who rules with power and authority over all. On bright days, like today, it seems Creator God Himself stands at the temple shining out His splendor across the land.

Qoricancha is the most important temple in the empire, and I am glad my family is blessed to live near it on the outskirts of the capitol city Cuzco. Here, holy things surround us with their protection.

My thoughts returned to the allyu. Preparations had begun for the evening meal.

Mother and Nana, her sister, placed bread made of ground quinoa, fresh avocado and chili peppers on a cloth on the ground. This will be our second and final meal of the day. We eat lightly in the morning, and a heavier meal around sunset. Corn and potatoes are the staples of our diet, but we also enjoy many other fruits and vegetables such as tomatoes, squash, pumpkin, and cactus fruit. On special days, we roast guinea pig or llama meat.

Unfolding my legs, I spread them out before me enjoying the feel of the stretch all the way down to my wiggling toes. As I rose from my manta, I heard the familiar tinkling of bells. Taruca is coming with the llamas.

My eight-year-old sister is a llamera and lots of fun. She spends her days tending the animals with other girls from our ayllu and the nearby village. The girls fill their hours on the hillsides inventing songs and dances to entertain themselves and their wooly, cud-chewing audience.

I always smile when I see Taruca leading Cusi, Inchic, and Mani, home from pasturing. She loves those funny looking beasts.

Skipping beside the llamas, Taruca urged the animals forward with sweet songs and friendly taps to their shaggy backsides. She entered the common area, her joyful spirit bubbling. "Huallpa, have you heard the news?" she asked breathlessly.

"What news? I've been working on my manta."
I lowered my lashes to hide my pleasure.
Taruca stopped and stared at me.

"You started your own?" she asked with childlike awe. Sometimes little sisters are good for a 13-year-old boy's heart.

"Yes," I said. "I will show you after we eat. Come, sit down and give us your news."

"I will, Brother. First I must put these willful creatures in their pen," Taruca said. She led the llamas to the enclosure behind our house and quickly returned, eager to relay her findings.

"Taruca, share your tidings," Mother said, peeling away the skin of an avocado and offering it to my cousin Totora. Only children eat this day. Adults fast in preparation for the upcoming festival.

With flashing dark eyes and lively gestures, Taruca began.

"Porters traveled past me on their way from the city. They were on the road, Hatun Nan, and their llamas were loaded down with provisions for the royal family in Machu Picchu. I heard them speak of plans for the festival."

"We were just discussing the Situa festival before you came," Mother said. "Tell us what you heard, Daughter."

"You know today is the day before the new moon, so the great Inca, Huayna Capac, met with his council at the temple to plan the celebrations for the festival. Inca is afraid for the people because there is much sickness across the empire. He and the council agreed the number of ceremonies should be increased this year."

Father nodded, then spoke quietly to his brother-in-law. "I have heard there are many sick in surrounding villages. This fever brings much pain. Blisters break out all over.

Young and old alike join the world of our ancestors. It is good to have more ceremonies."

Huallpa

CHAPTER 2

Situa

The Purification Festival

It is still dark outside. Sleep clouds my brain as I lay drowsily upon my mat. Thoughts of the day ahead urged me to leave the comfort of my warm blanket. I rose and stepped over sleeping Taruca, excitement coursing through my body and mind as I crossed the dirt floor and pushed aside the animal hide covering on the door of my family's home.

The mountains guarding our village came into view as my eyes began to focus. Slowly adjusting to the dim light, I strained to look beyond the thatch roofs of the neighboring stone buildings.

The morning of the feast day will dawn clear and bright in our city, though in the predawn light I see smoky rings circling mountain peaks at higher elevations. *The mountain gods must be pleased today.* I cannot hold back my smile on this day so full of promise.

A condor's cry pierced the morning stillness, and a shiver ran from my neck down to my toes. Surely this is a good sign. These great black birds are symbols of the things good people strive for, like calm and steadiness. They represent the hope of the future and the possibility that some day men and women will live in the spirit world soaring freely in the heavens.

Reluctantly, I turned to enter the house and prepare for the day. Mother greeted me at the door with a knowing look.

"Go, Huallpa," she said. "I will take care of the mats today."

She must remember the excitement of youth on festival days.

"Thank you, Mother," I called over my shoulder, and headed outside to the glorious day and its pledge of adventure. Taruca bolted out the door behind me, and we hurried to join our cousins buzzing about the common area like a hive of disturbed honeybees.

"I can't wait to see the soldiers in ceremonial clothes," Totora exclaimed.

"The dances are my favorite," chimed Taruca with a dip and a twirl.

"I want to see Huayna Capac in his royal garments and hear the ancient poetry," I said.

"My favorite is the food!" Guaman laughed and rubbed his belly with anticipation. "No matter what the festival is, you know there will be good food."

We all agreed this is true, but there is much more I am looking forward to other than filling my belly. Our little band scurried behind the houses to water the llamas that will stay in their pens this day.

Before leaving the ayllu, Father cut Taruca's forehead between her brows. He mixed her blood with cornmeal to break the fast of those who had not eaten the previous day.

Children must be between five and ten years of age to give the blood for the ritual food. Taruca was brave as the knife broke through her tender skin and blood spurted forth. Tears welled in her eyes, but she kept herself composed, understanding the importance of her role in the sacred ritual.

We began the short walk to Qoricancha with my uncles, aunts and cousins. Mother packed Pisco on her back tucked in the folds of her manta. Father, Taruca and I carried provisions and our household god to be blessed during the ceremonies.

Mother is wearing her usual costume — a one-piece wool dress reaching to her ankles and tied at the waist by an ornamental woven sash. Her dress, a large rectangle, is fastened at her shoulders with long pins. Parted in the center and secured by a woven headband, her uncut black hair hangs in a glossy sheet down her back.

Father wears his traditional breechcloth and a tunic reaching almost to his knees. Woven of one broad piece of coarse fibres, the fabric for the tunic is folded in half and stitched together along the side edges with the same brown thread used to make the material. An opening for the neck was created during the weaving, while holes for the arms were made when the piece was sewn. His manta drapes over his shoulders, and he carries a small bag tucked safely between the cloak and his tunic. Certainly, he would never travel to the city without his bag and its contents of dried coca leaves and amulets.

Like the other men in our community, Father crops his hair short in front. The back is somewhat longer and bound with a narrow decorative band. He and Mother wear sandals of untanned llama hide. Mine and Taruca's are made of woven grasses.

Crisp air nipped our faces as we walked in the morning shadows. Along the path, clusters of white lilies burst forth on sleek stems into cone-shaped blooms. They waved us on as we passed on the path from our village to the main route into the city.

The road became congested as we drew nearer to the meeting place, and the tide of my people rose upon the great golden temple. Thousands of dark eyes swam in a sea of bobbing brown faces.

I have to get nearer to the temple.

Breaking away from my family, I pressed forward into the swell of humanity, Taruca trailing behind.

In preparation for the festival, all people with physical defects had been sent out of the city. Dogs, whose howling is considered an evil omen, were put out as well. Any expected distractions or hindrances to the purification rites were purposefully removed from the area before the ceremonies began.

All was ready when the sun crowned the horizon, birthing the new day and silencing the noisy crowd. High Priest, Villa Umu, stepped out before the people. He wore ceremonial garments—a long red tunic reaching down to his ankles and hemmed with a wide band of decorative gold fringe. Metal masks embellished his leather sandals, and a wreath of feathers circled his head like rays shooting out from the sun.

"How greatly we have desired this festival." Villa Umu addressed the assembly. "Today is the day we have anxiously waited for — a day in which no man quarrels with his neighbor and no man goes hungry."

The High Priest delivered solemn instructions for the upcoming ceremonies. He spoke in the Quechua tongue used across the empire, known even by our captives whose rulers and common people integrate into our culture when conquered in battle.

"Let evils be gone, Oh Creator of all things, and allow us to see another year. May we be free from sickness, and may no diseases enter our homes," Villa Umu concluded then stepped backwards, making way for the reigning Inca.

Huayna Capac entered in regal splendor as Lord Sun's morning greeting lit up the golden temple behind him, a radiant confirmation of the Inca's divine nature.

A throng of thousands waited in complete stillness. No one spoke. No one moved.

Then Taruca slipped her small hand in mine. I felt her trembling. The same excitement surged through me, but I could not tear my eyes from the scene before me to look at her face.

Huayna Capac stood tall and commanding, robed in the finest red and purple vicuna wool, richly died and ornamented with gold and precious stones set in detailed embroidery. A collar of feathers billowed around his neck with each movement and breeze. Great golden medallions plugged his earlobes—they were three finger widths across and weighed down his lobes until they almost touched his shoulders. Metal bracelets encased his strong arms, each one a representation of bravery and valor. A necklace of the teeth of slain enemies dangled down his chest, and above it all, his noble head was crowned with the royal llautu, the headdress worn only by Sapan Incas.

Made of fine scarlet fabric with fringed edging, the llautu wrapped in many folds around his head. The headdress boasted two feathers standing upright within it of the rare and curious coraquenque bird. These feathers are the distinguishing sign of royalty, and a common man caught with one faces certain death.

Sapan Inca Huayna Capac lifted his powerful arms, bracelets tinkling, gemstones gleaming, and began the feast of Situa reciting the ninth Inca Pachacutec's words:

O, my Lord,
my Creator, origin of all,
diligent worker
who infuses life and order into all,
saying, "Let them eat,
let them drink in this world:"
Increase the potatoes and corn,
all the foods
of those to whom you have given life,
whom you have established.
You who orders,

who fulfills what you have decreed,
let them increase.
So the people do not suffer and,
not suffering, believe in you.
Let it not frost
let it not hail,
preserve all things in peace.[1]

This is a good prayer. Creator God can show how powerful He is by preventing the suffering of His children. When people do not suffer, they will believe in Him. He has been good to me. I will believe in Him.

When Huayna Capac finished speaking, all the people danced, even the mighty Inca, though he retreated after a short time into the golden shrine, Qoricancha. Jubilant music accompanied his departure as priests, clothed in embellished robes, played skillfully on trumpets and rang bells fashioned of brass and stone. Men sang out praises to the mighty Inca.

I returned Taruca to Mother and joined Father. Since my age is now 13 years, I am most eager to begin the ceremonies. This will be the first year I am allowed to participate in many of them. Rites and sacrifices will take place throughout the day, then the people will assemble again to await the arrival of the new moon.

As the moon came into view, the priests and all the people began shouting with great intensity. Over and over they whooped and cried . . .

Sickness, disasters and misfortunes get out of this land! Sickness, disasters and misfortunes get out of this land! Out of this land! Out of this land!

In the midst of the noise and commotion, people hit one other in sport with lighted straw torches. Those living in the city ran to their homes, arriving at their doors still bellowing the decree, *Sickness, disasters and misfortunes get out of this land! Out of this land!* Without entering the buildings, the city residents shook their clothing at the entranceways of their homes, a symbol that evil was being shaken from their dwellings.

Meanwhile, four hundred noblemen gathered in the heart of the capital square called Holy Place. They are Orejone, Big Ears, warriors with large metal plugs in their lobes, each plug bearing its own unique markings. Since it is a feast day, the warriors do not wear battle attire of quilted armor and basketwork helmets. Today they wear ceremonial dress — tunics of fine wool, sandals and embroidered sashes indicating their military rank. Adorning their heads, garlands of flowers and evergreens represent goodness, grace and endurance.

The orejone assembled at the intersection of the main roads — the point where passageways begin and spread out over the empire dividing the land into quarters. After splitting into four equal groups, in one great eruption, the warriors charged from the square, running down the streets, carrying their weapons and the cry of the priests.

Sickness, disasters and misfortunes get out of this land! Out of this land! Out of this land! This land!

In a great rush the men sprinted through the city intent on their mission to rid the area of evil. Waiting runners continued to relay the cry beyond the city boundaries until the last runners jumped, still shouting, in nearby rivers where they cleansed themselves and their weapons in the flowing waters. The river received the cry of the people. Its current swept evil away from the land into the sea.

When the runners finished, all the people washed, submerging themselves in the river — an outward demonstration of the spiritual cleansing taking place among us. I joined in the bathing and emerged from the cool waters chilled and hungry, but filled with anticipation for the coming year.

After the purification rite, we ate a bit of porridge made of coarsely ground maize. We smeared it on our faces, on the bodies of the dead, and around the doors in the city to symbolize the cleansing from evil. This closed the first day's rites.

Several days of dancing and feasting will follow, and more sacrifices will be offered upon the great altar. We are to receive lumps of maize flour mixed with llama blood. Four male llamas will yet be sacrificed — their lungs examined by the priests to determine if the year ahead will be prosperous.

Important men, princes and regional leaders from across the empire, will continue to gather at Qoricancha, bringing their idols and holy things for blessing and ceremonies. Chicha, a fermented drink made from maize, flows freely throughout the festival, and much merrymaking will take place as we celebrate the cleansing of our city and the entire empire.

Quipus

CHAPTER 3

Muru
The Death Pox

It is now 14 days past Situa. I noted their passing with knots tied on a quipus I made of spun and plied threads donated by Cusi, our best-natured llama. When my family and I returned from the festival, our spirits were high — as a condor in flight. Creator God received our many prayers offered with the animal and maize sacrifices. He must have seen how we worshipped and celebrated His abilities during the dances and rituals performed for His pleasure. Surely sickness and disease were carried away from our land by the river's swift current.

But why do I feel this way? My skin burns. My head hurts, and I am tired like I have never felt before. Over the last few days I pressed myself to sit up and finish my manta, but there is no strength left in my arms. Sitting takes more than I have within me — even though I would like to sit on the manta made by my own hands.

Strange visions carry me from place to place. My family fades in and out of them.

I am in the common area wrestling with Guaman. We sport with one other often. My cousin is stronger and usually pins me with ease, but this time I champion the match.

But what has happened? After I pinned him, Guaman disappeared, melting away to nothing in my grasp. I knelt on the dirt where we had struggled only a moment earlier. I am alone, with empty hands, clenching the air, wondering where he has gone.

Mother prepared tea from coca leaves, but I can no longer hold a cup. She dribbles small amounts into my mouth to ease my discomfort. I feel it going down my chin, but I cannot stop it.

The spots on my hands and forearms are filling with liquid, making painful bubbles on my skin. And something is happening inside my mouth. It hurts to swallow. I think I feel bumps in there, too. Has muru come to my house?

Hot. I am so hot. A cool cloth brushes over my damp brow rousing me from a restless sleep. I cannot press through to wakefulness.

Focusing is difficult. I hurt all over, both inside my body and on my flesh. Pisco cries in her cradle. *What is wrong with our "little bird."* Pisco learned to be quiet like a good Runa baby when the summer sun still shone brightly over the mountains. Something is not right.

I can't think of this now. I must close my eyes.

I have been dreaming again, but the haze in my head seems to be clearing. How much time has passed since I first lay down on my mat? The smells in the house are strong and things are not in order. Questions melt together in my heated skull.

I blinked my eyes. Taruca's sweet face floats above my head. There is an uncommon look about her that I do not understand.

"Huallpa," she said tenderly.

"Sister." My raspy voice sounded far away to my ears.

"You are here, Puric," she whispered. "You did not go to our ancestors in the spirit world."

"I am here," I croaked. "Water."

Taruca nodded and disappeared from view. I heard her bare feet padding across the dirt floor, then their return. Kneeling beside me, she placed her small arm beneath my head and held the gourd of water to my parched lips. Though my dry throat and mouth compelled me to gulp the soothing liquid, I sipped slowly, relishing the feel of it.

Exhausted, I lay back on my mat.

"You have slept many days," Taruca said solemnly.

"How many?"

"I am not certain of the number, but a lifetime passed in them."

"What do you mean? And why did you call me Puric? Where is Father? He is the head of the household."

"The men from the village buried him beside Mother and Pisco yesterday. Now you are Puric. I am your family, and you are my head."

I cannot think. This is too much. My brain is still clouded with sickness. That must be the reason Taruca's words confused me.

But she looks at me with those eyes. There is no shine in them today. Heaviness sits hard upon my chest, suffocating my spirit.

Muru has come, claiming many of my family in his greedy death grip. Carefully, I rose to sit. My back throbbed with pain. I am weak and scarred by pits, but alive.

Several days passed since I first awoke from the sickness. My strength is slowly returning. Taruca and I wander about our home and village without feeling or purpose. We feed and water the llamas. I cannot pick up the looms or shuttle vibrantly colored threads upon them.

Staying here without our family is too hard. I am thinking of a plan.

Was it only a month ago that Mother crushed and dried the potatoes into chuno? I watched Taruca use the white meal to make a spiced gruel to fill our uninterested stomachs. We sat quietly upon our mantas and prepared to eat the simple fare.

"Taruca."

She placed her spoon in her bowl and looked up at me with huge eyes.

"I feel we cannot stay here in our allyu. There are too many memories. We have lost so much, and I think it would be good for us to make a new beginning somewhere else."

She did not answer right away. I could tell she thought deeply of my words.

"I feel the same, Huallpa," she said softly. "I miss everyone so much. It is hard to bear staying here." She glanced around the empty allyu and then to me. "I still expect to see Mother and Father weaving on their mantas and Pisco bouncing beside them. But where would we go? What would we do?"

"I have a plan. We have three healthy llamas. They provide much fibres for weaving, but my heart refuses me to make our village patterns any longer. Let us take Cusi, Inchic and Mani to Machu Picchu. I have heard there is work there. Much building is yet to be completed and provisions need to be transported into the city. It is only a few days journey."

Taruca again sat in silence, thoughts swirling behind her dark eyes. I saw when her spirit settled within her.

"I will miss our home," she said, " but your plan is good. We can make a new start in Machu Picchu, and if we tire of life in the royal city, we can return. It is not too far."

Taruca's agreement gave me confidence to proceed with my plans. I had thought out many of the details already. "I will speak to Nana," I said. "She will watch over our house while we are away."

After speaking with Nana, Taruca and I spent the rest of the day deciding what to take with us. We rolled changes of clothing in Father's manta and selected the household and cooking items we thought we would need. Taruca packed several woven bags with herbs, dried vegetables and fruits, roots and nuts.

"Should we take this?" Taruca asked lifting our household god from the indentation in the wall.

I am not sure what is best, but I am Puric now. I laugh inside at the thought. *I am not a man to make such important decisions . . . but Taruca stands there with the image in her hand . . .*

"We will leave it here to watch over our home and allyu," I said with feigned composure. "Nana will feel better knowing the god of our ancestors stays with those who remain in the allyu."

Taruca placed the image back in the wall, accepting my answer, trusting in me.

Finally ready to sleep, we rolled our mats out upon the dirt floor of our home one last time.

"Huallpa," Taruca whispered in the darkness.

"Yes."

"Huallpa, I'm scared for tomorrow to come."

"If you were not, I would be surprised. I, too, am unsettled, but we will look upon it as an adventure. We will see new things and meet new people.

"You will have a new friend before the next full moon," I promised, hoping the thought would both distract and encourage her.

"I like to meet new people," she said, "but I am worried about the journey. You know how frightened I am of snakes, and we will be without shelter along the mountain trail."

"Before we reach the road to Machu Picchu, we will pass Sacsayhuaman where Father served in the army," I reminded her. "There is a temple in the fortress. We will ask the priests to sacrifice for us, and they will pray to the gods for our safe travel."

Taruca sighed and settled in for the night drifting off to sleep on the promises of a brother who worried enough for both of us.

The responsibility of caring for Taruca weighed heavily on my mind as I lay on the floor of the dark room listening to the night sounds outside the door. They did not comfort me as in the past.

I must rest.

I closed my eyes and joined Taruca in the land of dreams.

Taruca and Cusi

CHAPTER 4

Hatun Nan
The Road to Machu Picchu

I am thankful the rains have not yet descended from the sky. Dry season has not given way to the demands of heaven's tears to be released upon our lands.

We left our village early this morning. Taruca and I said our good-byes to Nana, Totora, and the rest of the family who survived muru's attack. It was not as difficult as I had imagined, for they walk as we do, in a cloud of grief that makes things happen in slow moving time and seem unreal.

The parting caused no tears. It seemed as if we were leaving only for a short trip and would return soon. With heavy arms, I gave Nana one last embrace, then Taruca and I turned to the path that would lead us away from our home. I could not leave without looking back — back to the ring of stone houses circling the grassy common area — to the vacant animal pen behind our house — to the pit where Pisco used to play.

My heart was heavy, but as we left I chose to think on new things and make plans for the future.

Quietly we walked along the path — Mani, Inchic and Cusi plodding beside us with our bundles secured to their backs. Bells tinkled softly, each animal's instrument creating a

37

unique tone that blended in a clinking, tuneless harmony. Lush greenery and fragrant flowers lined the way, but the scenic beauty and calming sounds did not penetrate the deep places in my heart and mind. I placed one foot in front of the other, veiled in a numbness that thinly covered the pain of recent loss.

We reached Sacsayhuaman in good time. "I remember talking to Father about this place." I said to Taruca as we approached the walled complex. "He learned much about the building of it when he served in the army."

"Tell me, Huallpa. I want you to tell me everything Father said."

"More than 20,000 men worked for 60 years to build this fortress. Those huge boulders were delivered from quarries far away, then craftsmen hammered them with river rocks. They chiseled precise joinings that fit the boulders together so perfectly a blade of grass could not squeeze in the gaps."

"The stones almost seem to grow together," said Taruca.

"Yes, and it looks like three men standing on top of each other would just reach the top of the tallest stones. I cannot imagine how heavy they must be."

"Our Incas are so full of wisdom to build such a place," said Taruca.

"I agree, Sister. Now you stay here with the animals and I will see if I can find the priest."

I left Taruca outside the fortress walls and located the priest in the temple.

"Pacco, " I concluded my story, "will you offer sacrifice and pray for our safe travel?"

"Yes, young man," the aging priest said. He took the measure of maize from my hands. "I would give you some advice as well. You may wish to join with other travelers on the road to Machu Picchu. It is many days journey, and you have your sister's safety to consider."

Nodding in agreement, I gave silent thanks Taruca tended our little herd outside the hearing of his words. "That would be wise, Pacco."

The priest accompanied me outside the fortress wall, stroking his furrowed chin as he walked. "Wait here," he said, then left me without further explanation.

Waiting was not long. I filled the time looking at the fortress and thinking how it was a key part of the capitol of the empire.

Cuzco is shaped like a puma, its map matching one of a twin cat drawn in the night sky by shining stars. My people carefully observe patterns in the stars, and Cuzco's shape is especially meaningful because we revere pumas for their great strength and fierceness.

Sacsayhuaman is the head of the puma named Cuzco. A sundial within the fortress is its exposed eye. The outer walls jut out along the perimeter like the jagged teeth of a wild cat.

The fortress is so large, in a time of conflict, all the people of the city could retreat inside. Perhaps that is why there is also a temple and great storehouses within the barricade, as well as underground passages to important buildings in the city. I have heard stories of people getting lost within the labyrinth passages, never to see daylight again.

The heart of the city and the great cat is the main square called "Holy Place." From this central plaza, four finely paved roads begin and spread out over the quadrants of the empire, arteries transporting people and resources throughout the land. A canal joins two rivers that make up the animal's tail, and golden Qoricancha glistens near the Holy Place in the location of the puma's reproductive organs.

Pacco returned. Three men came with him. As they drew close, I saw that two were grown, but one looked not much older than I. Dressed for travel, they walked steadily toward me. A big man, obviously their leader, looked me over then glanced across the way to Taruca and the llamas.

"What's your name?" the big man asked.

No word of greeting . . . and such a gruff manner. I wanted to shrink back from this man and his intimidating gaze, but I forced my eyes to stay connected with his.

"I am Huallpa, and my sister Taruca tends our llamas."

A guttural sound came out with an abrupt nod. He turned, and with a shrug of his broad shoulders passed a silent message to his traveling companions.

"I am Amaru. I pack provisions for the royal family to Machu Picchu. If you would like to travel with us, we can offer you protection. In exchange, provide us the backs of two of your llamas to transport goods to the city on the Old Peak."

With only a moment's consideration I gave my answer, "Yes, this is fair. I will speak to my sister."

"When the sun is at midday, bring your animals to the other side of the fortress and meet us on the road Hatun Nan. We will see you there," Amaru said. He motioned to his companions, and the group disappeared behind the fortress wall with Pacco.

I approached Taruca.

"Isn't it pretty?" she was asking Cusi in her silvery voice. She spoke of the orange flower she held for the llama to examine.

"Talking to llamas, Sister?"

"I always talk with Cusi. He is my favorite. He is sweet, and his color is unusual. The glossy black and white mix of his coat makes the most beautiful weavings," she boasted of her pet.

"Then we will give Cusi our personal items to carry," I told her. "We have been invited to join a group of porters who journey to Machu Picchu. Inchic and Mani will carry for them, and we will benefit from traveling with men familiar with the trail."

Happy with the news, Taruca playfully grabbed Inchic's shaggy head in her hands and shook it from side to side. The animal's big ears flopped and she snorted. Taruca scratched Mani between the ears and crooned to the females, "You little *peanuts* will work much harder as pack animals than you did grazing on the hillsides, but I suppose we must all make changes."

Her optimism cheered me.

"We will shift our belongings to Cusi after we have something to eat," I said, "then we meet our fellow travelers on the road to Machu Picchu."

Taruca opened Mother's manta and unwrapped the food prepared for our journey. Most of the dried vegetables and roots were secured on the llamas for the trip, but Nana had given a parting gift of food for us to eat along the way. We

41

selected squash and roasted guinea pig wrapped in cactus leaves, saving the rest of the manta's bounty for later.

While we ate, Taruca chattered. She babbled about the fort, the upcoming trip and everything else scampering through her brain or across her line of vision.

She noticed everything. Birds in the cacao trees. Clouds in the shape of a foot-plow . . . no, it's a goblet, don't I see that? A patch of coca plants across the way.

My mind, so full of questions, would have preferred quiet, but I responded to her words, glad she found adventure in this journey birthed in sorrow.

After our meal, we untied the bundles Inchic and Mani carried and tied them on Cusi's back.

"Sorry, Cusi," I comforted, "but you will be thankful for the lighter load when your friends are burdened down with provisions for the royal city."

"We must go," I said to Taruca, guiding Mani and Inchic away from the site of our meal. The llamas had partaken of the sweet grasses there as well, and we were all strengthened for the journey ahead.

Smiling, Taruca took Cusi's lead, and we set out on our way. The bells seemed to jingle more brightly as we headed to the road Hatun Nan.

Her smile did something to my heart, melting the edges of the hardened block inside my chest. Was it hope?

We arrived ahead of the men, but I could see them walking toward us. With the porters came many llamas bearing heavy burdens. Packs were also strapped on the backs of the men.

The younger man smiled at me. I am encouraged by his friendly face. Amaru is frightening.

"Ama sua, ama kjella, ama lllulla," the slender young man greeted me, still smiling.

This is good. Here is an authentic Runa. I smiled and returned the traditional greeting, "Don't lie, don't cheat, don't be lazy."

"I am Micos," he said. "I travel with Amaru and Chuchau to Machu Picchu."

"Huallpa. And this is my sister, Taruca. We are pleased to travel with you."

Amaru dropped the pack he carried and called to his companion. "Chuchau, bind our packs to that brown llama. Micos, take one bundle from each of our animals and put them on the other one. We leave right away."

I assisted Micos who introduced me to Chuchau, an average-sized man of middle age and even temperament. Inchic spat putrid green bile at Chuchau and voiced her displeasure at the weight and handling she was receiving, but Chuchau only laughed at her.

"You will carry my pack, hembra," Chuchau told the stubborn female. "Spit if you will, but it will not change your fate."

Taruca laughed—a pleasant sound to my ears.

"The only labor Inchic is accustomed to is growing shaggy fur used in our family's weavings," she said. "Her greatest burden has been the walk to and from the hillsides."

"Your animals will make our trip much easier," Chuchau confided. "Amaru should be less disagreeable without the weight of a pack on his back."

43

"I hope so," I said. Taruca's ears are not as big as her llamas', but they hear well. She looked up at me with concern on her face but kept her thoughts to herself.

We walked for several hours. I am thankful my health is returning. Taruca is strong and athletic. Time spent climbing and dancing on the hillsides readied her for this day. She sings the songs of the llameras as we travel the path to the river we must cross on the bridge called Cusichaca.

The suspension bridge made of dried, woven grasses hung between the river banks. Before we crossed, we prayed and offered small stones to River God. A large pile of similar offerings rose beside the bridge — memorials to the prayers of others who passed this way before us.

The crossing went without incident. We continued a short distance to where the river is noisy and fast flowing. The water looked inviting, so we stopped and allowed the animals to drink and to refresh ourselves, as well.

After the brief respite, we continued over level ground along the edge of the river, occassionally seeing a hut here and there. The pitch of the incline steepened, and plants grew more densely. In the aftenoon, we turned away from the river and faced our destination . . . the Old Peak.

Higher and higher we climbed, our surroundings changing along the way. The path took us through a small wooded area and then veered to the right over barren grasslands. When the ground became more difficult to cover, I looked back and saw the river valley far below.

Before reaching the first pass, we stopped for the night and prepared to camp under the stars.

CHAPTER 5

Mac'aqway!
The Snake

The second day of our journey brought us through Dead Woman's Pass. As we had done at the river crossing, we left stones beside the mountain passage before traveling through it. Mountain God controls much of our peoples' lives — sending water, making weather, and punishing with avalanches, storms and earthquakes.

We prayed and paid the small tribute then walked through the pass. Once clear, our party descended into the valley of Pacamayo where the trail began a steep upward climb from the valley to the next pass.

We walked in silence, our thoughts roaming as our feet rambled. Taruca's scream tore through our quiet musings.

"Mac'aqway! Mac'aqway!"

Taruca stood frozen on the path — her worst fear now her reality. One hand trembled at her throat while the other pointed to the grasses parting with mac'aqway's approach.

Our convoy came to an abrupt stop. Helpless to intervene, I watched. A venomous pit viper slithered toward my sister paralyzed by fear. *Oh, God, help her!*

Taruca had been walking before me. Two of Amaru's llamas separated us, but Micos was near her. He reached inside his garment, and deftly drew out several stones. With lethal precision, he pitched them at the yellow snake and hit the deadly reptile squarely on his lance-shaped head. Before the stunned snake could strike, Micos dashed forward and crushed its skull with his walking stick.

It took a moment before I began to breathe again. Everything happened so fast it hardly seemed real—except for the blood still racing through my body and the panic only starting to ease. I took a deep breath.

"Little Deer," I called to my shaking sister. (Mother called Taruca "Little Deer" when she was younger.) She looked at me, then ran to my side, eyes bulging like the medallions in Huayna Capac's ears.

"You are brave, Little Deer."

"Huallpa, I was so scared," she said, breathless and still trembling. "You know how snakes have always frightened me. From the cradle I have feared them."

Running my hand from the top of her head down her fall of black hair, I spoke words I hoped would reassure her.

"Today you faced your fear on this path, and you were not struck down. The gods smiled on you once again. You are the only one of our family untouched by muru, and you are safe today from a poisonous snake that could have taken your life."

"We will stop here to rest," said Amaru.

My opinion of the gruff man is improving. *Perhaps Taruca's sweet songs softened his heart*, I thought, thankful he allowed some time for Taruca to recover before traveling on.

I offered food from Mother's manta to our companions while Taruca washed her face from a bladder of water filled at the spring. She checked the ground carefully then plopped down on a fallen log exhausted from her traumatic encounter.

With pleasure, Taruca soon learned Micos carried more than rocks within his clothing. He pulled a wooden flute from his pouch and played the soothing music of our people. The wind in the wood whispered quiet back into our spirits.

We continued our journey, stopping at a tambo the second evening. At the courier post we found sleeping quarters and pens for our animals. Taruca especially enjoyed the shelter. Surely she would be safer from snakes here, she reasoned.

Our third day traveling brought us to Town-in-Steep-Place. After descending to the valley floor and crossing it, we began another climb that led us to a tunnel, a natural opening in the rock widened by Runa laborers. Even our animals passed through without difficulty.

Cloud-level Town, the site of magnificent ceremonial baths, was next on our journey. A network of interconnecting stone towers, fountains and stairways spilled down the mountainside amid vibrant orchids, mosses and ferns. A spring high above the cloud forest fed the baths enjoyed by nobility and common alike. All have access to the baths, a person's rank in society determining what level of bath they may enter.

After Cloud-level Town, we passed through Forever Young. Taruca delighted in this place named for the pretty pink orchids growing in abundance.

"We'll stop here," said Amaru.

Taruca, pleased with his decision, hurried past the level campsite to the colorful butterflies fluttering across the trail. A good spot for our last night on the road Hatun Nan.

Darkness joined us. Taruca and I lay close together upon our mats near the crackling fire. Nights are cold in the mountains, so we wrapped ourselves in warm blankets made by loving family members who no longer needed them.

"Wh . . . wh . . . what is that?" Taruca asked.

"What do you speak of? I heard nothing."

"I did. O . . . Over there. B . . . By the rocks."

"I think your meeting with the mac'aqway has made you as nervous as an old woman."

"Please, Huallpa," she pleaded. "Will you see what it is?"

Reluctantly, I rose from my mat, took a stick from the fire to light my way and walked in the direction Taruca indicated. As I neared a rock pile, I heard the noise causing her concern. It was faint, but growing louder . . . chirp . . . Chirp . . . CHIRP!

Movement flashed in the corner of my eye. I turned my head to see a silvery gray fur ball jump from the top of the rock pile to the ground by my feet—a dense ball of fur with big round ears and eyes. The chirping intensified to a loud barking noise, and the animal reared up on its tiny feet.

Without warning, a warm spray hit my ankles.

What is that? I wondered in shock before understanding came.

Uggh! A chinchilla peed on my leg!

I stepped back in disgust. Perhaps this nocturnal rodent did not welcome my bright torch, but I did not appreciate his expression of displeasure.

I snatched a bit of cloth from Father's bag which I now wore tied around my neck and hastily wiped off the offense. "Chinchilla pee. Unbelievable." I muttered all the way back to the campfire where my bravery was heralded only by the sound of Taruca's regular breathing. She slept.

Micos approached as I settled on my sleeping mat again. "Tomorrow we shall see the day break at the Gateway of the Sun," he said.

With great anticipation I look to the morning and the Gateway of the Sun. Creator God made Lord Sun to light and nourish the earth, and tomorrow I will stand in his gateway as he enters the great city of Machu Picchu.

We awoke early, gathered our belongings in the dim light and lead the llamas back on the trail for the last leg of our journey. From scrub and woodland, the path quickly changed, dropping into a cloud forest that delivered us to a steep flight of stone steps. We mounted the narrow stairway and began our climb through the mist to the Gateway of the Sun.

Compared to other Runa buildings, like Qoricancha or Sacsayhuaman, the Gateway's looks are not impressive.

Location and unique function make it special. Two large stone structures curve around a circular grassy floor on the peak of the old mountain and create openings both sunbeams and travelers pass through to enter Machu Picchu.

The royal city lies in the distance, well below the Gateway. Twice each year on winter and summer solstices, a shaft of light forms through the Gateway, travels down the mountain, across the city, and (depending on the season) passes directly through either the left or right window of the Temple of the Sun. Light spills across the temple's altar where priests perform sacrificial rituals during festive celebrations. The abilities of men to plan, obtain materials and build such a precise formation on top of a mountain is more than my mind can understand.

Our band of travelers arrived at the site before Lord Sun. Silently, expectantly, we awaited the approach of the great day star.

As we tarried, my eyes roamed the mystical beauty surrounding this sacred place. Though the light was yet dim, I was still able to make out the fertile Urubamba Valley and the river of the same name tearing its way through the canyon far below. Beyond the river, an immense green jungle stretched out before distant mountains wearing snowy caps plumed with misty fringe.

In one transitional moment, bright beams slipped through the entrance of the Gateway. Lord Sun's touch crept across the land to awaken the slumbering city below. Light inched down the mountain that towered behind the city then advanced upon the buildings. Bit by bit, Machu Picchu's exquisite details unveiled as a blaze of morning glory burned away the night and illuminated the settlement tucked away among the mountains.

Taruca slipped her hand in mine and smiled up at me. My thoughts replayed a similar occasion . . . at Situa . . . when we shared another sunrise . . . before . . .

Amidst the flush of morning light, sorrow and hope mingled in my heart. I thought of the joy our family shared at the last purification festival—my first celebration with Father as I passed from boyhood to become a man—before muru stole him, Mother and Pisco away to Hanan Pacha. Some day Taruca and I will meet them in the spirit world, but until then, I must look to our future.

I admired the royal city below and wondered what lay ahead for us this morning and in the days to come. Gazing upon Machu Picchu, I allowed myself to hope that this sanctuary for the nobility and priesthood also held promise and provision for Taruca and me.

We delayed our descent until Lord Sun's radiance covered the entire city, then we rose and moved down the granite stone trail.

Chinchilla

CHAPTER 6

Machu Picchu
The Royal Retreat

Our party descended as Machu Picchu bathed in sunshine. Perched far above the Urubamba Valley and hidden by surrounding mountains and jungles, this retreat of the royal family is both safe and beautiful.

The city is being constructed with elaborate planification. Stone terraces and buildings were designed in harmony with the terrain of the Old Peak. Surely we are closer to the gods here, and safer from enemies. I see Inca's face looking to the sky in the sculpture of the mountains.

Details came into focus as we neared the city. Building openings — walls, doors and windows — all inclined inwardly at the top. My curiosity aroused, I questioned Chuchau.

"Why are the doors and windows constructed in this odd shape?"

"City planners believe buildings withstand earth shakings better when walls and openings slant in at the top," Chuchau answered.

"I see."

We continued on, and I surveyed the layout of the city. A rectangular courtyard serves as centerpiece, with a huilca tree rising from the middle of the lush green floor. This special tree is important to the priests who use it to make an intoxicating snuff for religious ceremonies. Inca sees visions under its effects.

Three unique sectors built of beautifully grained white stonework surround the courtyard. These sectors wear skirts of stone terraces notched into the contour of the sloping mountainside.

"We take our goods to the Royal District," Amaru said, breaking through my wandering thoughts. "Coya's envoy will meet us there to receive them."

"Is Huayna Capac in the city?" I asked. I hoped to see the Sapan Inca again.

"No. After Situa, he left Cuzco and took much of the royal family to Quito," Chuchau said. "Coya is here, Inca's mother, Mama Ocllo."

Taruca's eyes flashed excitement with the news of royalty in the city.

"Come, Taruca," I said, feeding the little girl's hopes with my cojoling words and smile, "you may see nobles today."

We continued our trek. Passing through the Sacred District, Micos pointed out the various holy things and important places.

"That is the Hitching Post to the Sun, Intihuana," he said as we passed the hallowed stone pillar.

"This is where the priests determine the time of the celestial periods," I explained to Taruca. "Twice a year at midday the sun stands directly above the pillar and makes no shadow at all. When this happens, the sun sits with all its might upon the pillar and is tied to this rock. It is a holy place."

"I have heard of the power of Intihuana," Taruca said. She touched her head to the granite stone with reverence, seeking a vision into the spirit world.

We moved on, leading our animals to the Royal District where we will lighten their burdens and complete our journey.

"The wise men and nobles stay here," Chuchau said. He motioned to rows of houses grouped together on a slope. Amaru stopped our convoy a short distance from the polished stone buildings.

"Stay here," he commanded, then walked away, disappearing in one of the entranceways.

As we waited, Taruca stroked Cusi's silvery gray hair and sang llamera songs in his pointy ears. I stood next to her drinking in the sights and sensations of Machu Picchu. Swinging about the city from one pleasure to another, my eyes took in the masterful craftsmanship, the power and enchantment emanating from the city.

Neither the brilliance of Qoricancha's golden temple, nor the imposing fortress of Sacsayhuaman, compare with the profound artistry of this place. An enormous beauty, Machu Picchu perfectly unites human workmanship and the rare natural setting of the mountain residence. The jewel of the Incas sparkles before me.

One by one, a group of women, young and old, stepped through the slanted door of a building in the complex Amaru had entered. Embroidered clothing of fine, dyed wool revealed their nobility and wealth.

One of the women, an older lady, looked our way. She spotted the animals loaded with provisions and nodded her head in approval. When her eyes found my Taruca, a strange look passed over her face.

She spoke in a low voice to a young woman beside her. Concern bubbled in my belly as the noblewoman's attendant began walking toward us.

Taruca saw her coming and stepped closer to my side.

With the agility of a deer, the young woman crossed the grassy knoll. She wore kindness on her pretty face, and when she stood before me, plump berry lips spoke words that traveled slowly to my brain.

"I am Pacari," she said, tipping her mass of blue-black hair in greeting. "Coya wishes to speak to this girl."

Coya! We are standing before the queen mother of great Huayna Capac . . . and she wishes to see Taruca. I tried to hide my surprise and show Taruca no expression to give her concern.

"I am Huallpa," I said, my eyes locking with the woman's black almonds. "This is my sister."

"Taruca, please go with Pacari and speak to Coya as she wishes."

Nodding, Taruca walked away with Pacari, glancing over her shoulder with questions on her innocent face.

I was surprised as I observed their interaction. I tried to keep from staring, but could not tear myself away from the scene that played out before me. Coya's attendants brought mantas for her and Pacari to sit on. She spoke to Taruca who opened Mother's manta (now empty of food) and joined them on the grass.

Coya seemed to enjoy Taruca. She smiled and looked into her eyes as my sister spoke. When she talked to her, she touched Taruca softly on the shoulder, the same way Mother used to do when her little girl was anxious. Taruca seemed calm in Coya's presence. After four days on the trail with llamas and odorous men, she warmed easily to the attentive women.

Amaru returned with several men. They unloaded the packs from the llamas and carried away the provisions. I made certain our personal things remained on Cusi—all this accomplished between covert glances at the gathering across the way.

Pacari rose and came to me again.

"Mama Occlo enjoys your sister. She reminds her of her granddaughter, Urpi, who was taken to the spirit world."

"We too have lost many to Hanan Pacha," I said, conscious of the pits the sickness dug into my face. "Muru took Mother and Father and our baby sister not long after the feast of Situa."

Tenderness crossed Pacari's poised face before she spoke again.

"Taruca says your family are weavers."

"Yes, those in our ayllu worked with the fibres of these llamas."

Pacari stroked Cusi's elongated neck. "Fine animals."

"Taruca showed us your mother's manta. It is well made. The wool is of high quality and spun with expert craftsmanship. The colors are bright and uniform—the threads even, and the pattern intricate and beautiful."

Her praise was pleasing. It warmed my face.

"Our home is here, near the priests," Pacari continued, indicating the red-walled buildings on the other side of the grassy knoll. She paused and considered her next words before speaking again.

"Muru claimed many of the Chosen Women responsible for weaving textiles used in the temple. Coya is lonely. Her son has taken most of the royal family to Quito, but she is too old to make the trip. Taruca would be a comfort to her."

Taruca would be a comfort to her? What is she saying?

"Coya has asked me to speak with the priests to request your sister begin training as one of the Chosen Women. She would be under their protection and continue your family's tradition of weaving beautiful textiles. Having Taruca near would comfort the queen. She is a sweet girl, and looks very much like Coya's lost Urpi."

What can I say? What can I do? My Taruca is summonsed by Mama Ocllo.

"I will speak to Taruca," I said, struggling to contain a surge of emotions. It is an honor to be a Chosen Woman. I should be happy for Taruca, but I think of my aloneness and wonder what my future holds.

Will the priests treat her well? Will I be allowed to see her? She is my last family member.

Where will I stay? What will I do without her?

What is life like as a solitary person with no family to share it?

Pacari looked deeply into my eyes and saw the feelings I struggled to hide but could not deny.

"What will you do?" she asked.

"Taruca and I came to Machu Picchu to make a fresh start. I heard there is building to be completed here." I shrugged my shoulders and lifted the tone of my voice. "I did not imagine Taruca would be employed before me."

My feeble smile convinced neither of us of my good humor. After a few awkward moments, Pacari spoke.

"Sinchi is the chief builder. Though the fountains and channels are complete here and in the Sacred District, work remains throughout the rest of the city. You will find him on the other side of the courtyard past the Hitching Post of the Sun," she said. "Perhaps he will find work for you."

"Thank you. I will go there after seeing Taruca settled."

Pacari glided back across the grass, her last words replaying in my spirit, "God be with you."

Pacari

CHAPTER 7

Sinchi
The Chief Builder

Leaving Taruca with the priests was more difficult than leaving our allyu had been. There we left the dead, but my sister is alive and depending on me to look after her. But we must leave in Hanan Pacha those who have gone to the higher world of paradise, and we must care for the needs of the present world in which we live. This is the Runa way — each day taken for what it has to offer.

My sister seems at peace with the women and priests. She settled comfortably in her new quarters and will learn the trade of our family. Her days will be full.

The demand for textiles is great. New clothes must come with each sunrise to adorn the great Inca. After only one wearing, his elaborate garments are burned. Much effort is spent clothing our divine emperor.

"I will check on you when the sun sets," I told Taruca before I left to find work.

On my way to locate Sinchi, I passed a man and a woman, both stripped of their clothing and very near death. They were tied by their hands and feet to a stone wall. It is unusual to see this type of punishment. Crime is not common in our culture — the penalty too great. Anyone insulting the gods or the Sapan Inca is thrown from a cliff. I once saw a man without hands — they had been cut off as penalty for stealing — but never have I seen adulterers tied to a wall to die of starvation and exposure.

Many flights of stone steps create pathways throughout the city, some carved from single blocks of granite. I arrived at the top of one of the stairways and saw men working on channels to provide water in this sector.

"Is Sinchi here?" I asked a laborer chiseling a hole in a great rock.

"He works at the fountain," the man answered. He rose from his work and showed me the way.

I crossed the stone path and walked with an anxious niggling in my chest to join the man the laborer indicated. *How will he receive me?* I wondered. *Will I find work in the city, or be forced to return to the allyu alone?*

"Ama sua, ama kjella, ama lllulla," I said as Sinchi rose upon my approach. "I am Huallpa. I have come to Machu Picchu looking for work."

"Don't lie, don't cheat, don't be lazy," Sinchi answered. His dark eyes looked me over from head to toe.

"What type of work do you do?"

"My people weave textiles, but I look for a new trade. Muru took most of my family. I do not wish to work the looms any longer."

We shared a moment of silence, each appraising the other. Sinchi looked just as I had imagined he would — lean and muscular, but showing the years spent laboring in the sun.

He appeared to be around Father's age, but I knew that although I had the advantage of youth, I would swiftly lose a wrestling match with this sinewy man.

Calling back my straying thoughts, I realized that Sinchi did not seem the sporting type. I could not think of gaming with the master mason before me. His face was neither harsh nor friendly as he turned his gaze to the sacred plaza.

"You know Inca determines the trades of his subjects," he reminded me.

"Yes, Sinchi," I answered. The hope that had risen in my chest slumped down to my sandaled feet.

Sinchi nodded. I held my breath through his next lengthy pause.

"Did you consult the priests in your region before coming to Machu Picchu?" he asked, still looking at the Temple of Three Windows.

"Yes." I breathed again. "My sister and I stopped at Sacsayhuaman before we began our journey. Pacco said prayers and offered maize for us."

Sinchi nodded, then turned to face me.

"Have you experience with tools?"

"Some," I said. "I am willing to learn if you are willing to let me try."

Sinchi nodded a third time, this time with consent in his dark eyes.

"We work on the last of 16 channels bringing water to the city from the holy spring. I will explain how we split the stones."

Curious about the process, I listened intently to Sinchi's explanation.

"First we hammer a row of holes in the great stones with chisels. Next, we wedge plugs of wood tightly into the holes and wet them thoroughly. When the wood dries, it swells, cracking the granite boulders in a straight line, from hole to hole. We are then able to divide the stones with levers."

"I often wondered how the laborers prepared the stones for setting in the massive walls," I said, admiring the skill and intelligence of the people.

"This is the easy part," Sinchi said. "The hard part is getting them up the mountain."

"I have heard stories of hundreds of men using ramps to move boulders from the quarries to the mountain tops."

"Sometimes thousands of men are required to transport one great stone," Sinchi added.

"Where are you staying, Huallpa?"

"My sister stays with the priests in the Royal District. She trains to make textiles for use in the temple. If I find work, I will stay in the Popular District where our llamas are being kept."

"That is good," Sinchi said. "Let us see if you are to be a builder, Huallpa. Try the chisel here."

I took the tool made of rock in hand. It felt comfortable in my grasp. *I can do this.*

I labored until Sinchi called us to break for the evening meal. Yancuna women served thick vegetable stew to fill the empty bellies of hardworking men. I had never been so hungry and consumed every remnant of food placed before me. I could have eaten more.

As I ate, I remembered the days spent in the common area of the ayllu. Work then was pleasureful with family, and not as hard on the muscles of my upper body and hands. My legs ached from squatting.

We resumed our work, and the women who served us began a song.

"What do they sing?" I asked Sinchi.

"It is called *Yarqha Haspi*," he said. "It is sung only while work is performed on the canals. Providing water for the city is important work. The women sing for us as we labor."

The song moved my attention from my blisters and weariness to the good the canal will bring. *This water will bless the royal family for generations to come.*

My mind turned to Taruca. I wondered how she was doing with her lessons. She is a good girl. I smiled thinking of her. Now that Mother and Father are gone, it will be my responsibility to find a husband for her if the priests allow her to marry.

She is very young, and although she seems to have found a secure place, I still feel the weight of her future upon me. She is beautiful, unmarked by the disease that swept through the land taking so many lives and scarring so many others. Many men would wish to have her with her sweet nature and fair looks.

The sun crept slowly across the sky until it was finally time to leave. I was anxious to check on my sister.

"Come back tomorrow, Huallpa," Sinchi said. He grinned at me then added, "if you can walk. You worked hard today. You will learn to build because you desire to do so."

"I will be here."

Sinchi is a wise man. He knew I worked through pain the last part of the day. He was pleased.

I crossed the courtyard to the Royal District hoping to find Taruca, and perhaps Pacari.

Pacari captured my thoughts again. Her face and figure danced before me in the secret place of my mind. Was it only a few hours ago that I had never known her? And now she is part of my inner voice, speaking to me from across the city. I wonder if she thought of me this day.

CHAPTER 8

Capacocha
The Sacrifice

Daily rain spills from the sky shortening the number of hours I toil with Sinchi's laborers. Today's downpour caused work to be delayed and provided the opportunity for me to visit Taruca. I miss my little sister and look forward to seeing her.

Large, translucent raindrops penetrated my clothing with cold jabs, and a shivers raced down my back. I lifted my manta over my head and hurried along the familiar stone path that led to the Royal District.

Although I walked quickly, I enjoyed the sights along the way. I never tire of the beauty of Machu Picchu. The great city rests between two mountains on the edge of the rainforest jungle. All around, towering green peaks, some shrouded in mists, appear to watch over this mystical place. Not far from the path, brilliant wild orchids grow among the dense vegetation. Mosses and ferns dot the landscape with texture and hue, while hummingbirds dart back and forth among fragrant, flowering trees.

The moon has completed two phases since we entered the city. It seems good that Taruca and I came to Machu Picchu.

My fellow laborers and I finished work on the last channel. Water flows throughout the complex. Now workers have begun carving additional terraces into the side of the mountain. Terracing prevents soil from washing away in the heavy rains that come to this region each year and also enables the planting of more crops. More crops grown on city terraces means less provisions packed up the trail.

Amaru may have to learn farming, I thought to myself with a grin.

It feels good to jest, if only to myself. I am beginning to enjoy the new life I have found here.

As I walked along, my thoughts turned to my sister. Pacari reports that Taruca spins fibres well and has won the favor of the priests. She will begin instruction on weaving temple textiles soon.

I have observed Coya's tender expressions toward Taruca. They speak many words unsaid. My sister brings joy to Mama Occlo in the absence of the royal family.

I've been lost in thought, I realized, dropping my arms to my side. How long ago did the rain cease and yet I still held my manta overhead?

In the distance, the tip of a rainbow caught my attention. I left the path to get a better view of the magnificent colored arc wedged beneath the city between two mountains. What a sight, to look down upon a rainbow. After filling my eyes, I returned to the trail and continued the short walk to the Royal District.

"Chasqui came today!" Taruca exclaimed, rushing toward me as I entered the Royal District.

She must have been watching for me. I am glad she thinks of me, as I think so much of her when we are parted.

Pacari followed the vibrant girl who raced across the courtyard bursting with her report. I looked from the girl to the woman behind her. One smiled, one did not.

"Chasqui brought fish for Coya," Taruca continued. "She said I will share some with her during the evening meal. It is a long time since we have eaten fish."

Smiling at her enthusiasm, I agreed, "Fish are a treat on top of this mountain.

"You must be thankful to have time with Coya away from your work in the temple."

"Yes," Taruca agreed. "The priests are kind, but I am accustomed to being free to run on the hillsides with the llamas. When Coya asks for me, my heart and feet jump together to be with her in the sunshine."

Taruca spread her arms wide and spun about in pleasure. Her glowing face lifted to drink in the sun as her dark hair swung out freely behind her.

"I am glad you are treated well, Sister. And I am thankful also for the break the rains gave me to visit you today."

Turning my attention to Pacari, I asked her the question burning within me. "Did the runners also bring news from the city?"

"Yes," said Pacari. "Bearded men with white faces have come to our land on floating wooden houses. They invade our coasts and the people are afraid."

This is certainly new and curious information. Legend says Creator God appeared in the form of a white-faced, bearded man — that after He created the earth and its gods, He traveled across the great water. Has He returned with new sons to rule over us?

"That is not all," Pacari continued. "Word has also come that Huayna Capac is mortally ill. It is feared muru battles for Sapan Inca's life.

"Coya mourns already for her son and the empire that is split in two by Huayna Capac's decision to divide the kingdom between his two sons, Atahualpa and Huascar.

"The High Priest from Cuzco sent word that special sacrifices are to be offered in every temple across the land. These will take place in two days when the moon is full."

"It is wise to beseech the gods in such times," I said.

"It is wise to offer sacrifices and prayers to One who can help," she replied in a voice I have never heard her use before. She is upset. I am confused.

Pacari bewilders me at times with her talk of the One God. She says He is Creator God, and this I understand. But she does not worship Lord Sun, his wife the Moon Goddess, the Thunder God, the Earth God, or any of the other gods and goddesses of the people.

Pacari's usual peace has fled, and in her disturbance, my soul spins with hers, uncertain where it will land when the spinning stops.

"Taruca, would you please bring your brother some refreshment?"

"Yes, I will," she answered. "I will bring you a cool drink of chicha, Huallpa. Would you like some, too, Pacari?"

"No, but thank you, Little One."

Humming one of her merry llamera songs, Taruca left us to retrieve the drink from inside the building.

"What's wrong, Pacari?" I asked.

"Huallpa," she replied with urgency in her voice, "we must consider that muru took many of the Sun Virgins and Chosen Women. When Huayna Capac became Inca after his father, 200 children were sacrificed."

"What are you saying, Pacari?"

"That I am concerned for Taruca. We have a small population in Machu Picchu, especially few children. Your sister is so sweet and beautiful the priests may think of her as a pure offering sure to satisfy their gods."

"I did not think of this type of sacrifice," I admitted to her. I had thought only of a llama's blood spilled on the sacrificial altar, but there are times when a greater offering must be given.

"It is an honor to be chosen for such a noble sacrifice, Pacari."

"Huallpa, the blood of strangled girls will not appease gods of natural elements nor those fashioned of gold. Creator God does not wish this."

Taruca returned with the chicha.

"Thank you," I said, and sipped slowly, considering Pacari's words. My sister is all that remains of my family. I don't want to think of losing her, but isn't the good of the empire more important than my personal loss? The gods are great and mighty. They hold the lives of all in their hands. We must pay homage to those who sustain and protect us.

I am thankful I am not the one to make such a grave decision. "We will see what the priests decide."

How did she know? I wondered as the full moon rose overhead. Even Coya's pleas had not changed the minds of the temple priests. Their power is great. In the capitol city of Cuzco, High Priest Villa Umu's authority is rivaled only by Sapan Inca's. The priests of Machu Picchu dominate this city in the same way and maintain strict control over the sacrifices performed in their region.

Taruca led the procession seated upon a golden litter as we marched to the Royal Mausoleum — a carved statue with a vault used for rites of sacrifice. I walked with the column of participants, solemn yet accepting of the forthcoming events. As the only family member of the capacocha, the child sacrifice, I am honored to be included in the procession.

After ceremonial baths and preparations, Taruca was dressed in fine clothing suitable for nobility. Being chosen for the sacrifice transforms an ordinary girl into royalty. Taruca will be honored with the death of a princess.

She wears a beautiful robe woven in a brilliant pattern of gold, red, white and purple. Delicate embroidered moccasins cover her once dancing feet, now folded carefully beneath her. Copper bracelets encase her wrists, and a shawl wraps her small shoulders squared to greet her fate with dignity.

Taruca's long hair is plaited in more than 200 braids and secured by layers of a black llautu wrapped about her head. Fringes of wool threads edging the headdress mask her dark eyes, and a crown of colorful feathers circles about her head.

Red and yellow pigments color her smooth face in ceremonial blush.

Arriving at the monument, attendants transferred Taruca from the litter to a wooden stool, her new moccasins never touching the earth's soil. She holds a small bag of nail clippings, hair and teeth to carry with her to the spirit world.

Bedecked in fine clothing and ornaments, the most comely thing about Taruca is not her manmade covering or preparations, but her natural grace and composure. It is undeniable, shining forth to all gathered to partake in the rite of the capacocha.

I thought back to the day Father took blood from Taruca's forehead before the Situa festival. She had been brave then, as she is now. I am proud to be with her.

In preparation for the ceremony, Taruca had drunk much chicha, emptying the contents of a golden, jewel-studded goblet several times before the procession began. It seems she is beginning to feel the numbness as she sits with heavy eyes upon the stool she will spend her next life upon.

The priest began the ceremony. It is hard to pay attention to his words as I stare at my sweet sister.

He wrapped the cord around her small neck, and with a strong arm, pulled it tight, offering my little deer to the gods. I pray they receive the sacrifice.

Although it is an honor and I am to be thankful to be part of the chosen family, my own breathing suddenly became difficult as Taruca took her last breath. Outwardly I must not show the turmoil brewing inside, but how I will miss my sister.

Taruca will be buried on the little stool — encased with fine weavings and a golden llama accompanying her on her journey to Hanan Pacha. In my mind I named the figure Cusi. Taruca will not be alone in her burial chamber.

Pacari came to me weeping.

"I begged the priests to take me instead of Taruca, but they would not hear of it," she gasped between the sobs that racked her slender shoulders. "They insisted the sacrifice come from the temple and said I am needed to serve Coya."

I wondered at her words. They make no sense to me. Taruca was honored in her death, a death Pacari despises. Why would she offer to trade places with her?

I could not keep my hand away. I touched her arm then asked in a whisper, "Why, Pacari?" Pushing back a veil of dark hair, I studied the depths of her sorrowful eyes. "Why would you trade places with Taruca if you think the capacocha is offered in vain?"

"You would not understand," she said, then turned and ran to her dwelling.

She is right. I do not understand.

CHAPTER 9

Pacari
The Comforter

More chasqui relayed grave news from Quito. All construction has ceased.

Muru delivered the soul of Huayna Capac, our divine Sapan Inca, to the world of our ancestors.

Coya will not be comforted. The death of her son pushed her spirit into a dark place. She spends her days surrounded by mindful attendants, yet desperately alone in her great sorrow.

Deprived of family and Taruca's joyful songs to cheer her, Mama Ocllo languishes within the confines of her trapezoidal chamber, out of the sight of the people and Lord Sun. The vulturous talons of hopelessness grasp tightly about her heart.

Pacari ministers to her. She tells me Coya will not eat, even refusing the chocolate and popped corn she entices her with.

Severe circumstances have scattered our people accustomed to the secure government of authoritarian Inca rule. Grief amplifies the anxiety of those gathered about our Coya. I am glad Pacari is here for her . . . and for me.

I stay now in the dwelling of the priests. After Taruca's sacrificial death, the priests honor me in this way. I am the only family of the capacocha and am rewarded for Taruca's gift to the gods. But how I would take the smelly llamas for roommates again to have my sister back.

Living now in the Royal District, I often see Pacari. Something within me responds to this woman. I search for opportunities to be with her. My eyes thirst to drink in her lovely countenance. I have memorized her features, replaying them for myself, one by one, in torturous treasure, longing to be with her beyond my secret thoughts.

Raven hair cascades in glossy sheets from Pacari's noble forehead. Finely sculpted brows and curling lashes frame kind, dark eyes. High cheekbones turn to apples when she smiles, and the curve of her full lips is pleasant. Her neck is graceful, her hands and feet, also.

When I think of Pacari, shining thoughts fill my empty hours — hours that used to be filled with work and the company of my sister.

There is more that draws me to this woman than physical beauty. Pacari carries a peace that calls to me. It confuses me, too. When I am in her presence, I feel both calming and stirring in places I did not know dwelt within me. Even my body reacts when she is near, quickening the beats of my heart.

Pacari is thoughtful and intelligent. I enjoy the conversations we share. We talk about many things.

I tell her stories of my allyu — describing for her how the shaggy llamas looked after Father took their wool — like overgrown wet cats.

I recalled when once, curious Cusi was bitten on the nose by a snake. Luckily, it was not poisonous, but it did frighten Taruca terribly.

Pacari especially enjoyed one story of unusual bravery, Taruca's great adventure in the pastureland. On a quiet afternoon, Mani grazed lazily upon the hillside with Inchic, Cusi and a herd of sheep tended by Cousin Totora. A fox sought to cut a lamb from the fold, targeting it for an easy meal. Usually docile Mani shocked Taruca when she sprung to action. With amazing accuracy, the llama spit a smelly green blob on the attacking animal's face. The fox stopped in its tracks. Then Mani sat on it, crushing its rib cage and saving the day.

Pacari tells me of the splendor within Inca palaces and baths. I have seen the scalding overflow from the baths filling the air with vapor, but never have I entered a royal chamber. Tending Coya has provided many opportunities for Pacari to witness things most Runa people never see.

Pottery fascinates Pacari. She prefers whistling pots shaped like animals, especially jaguars and llamas. As a child, she spent much time watching artisans shape and paint the decorative vessels.

Her expressive eyes softened when she told of dancing the *Wayllacha* at a family celebration. She had been near Taruca's age, and the group dance shared with visiting kin held special memories for her.

Pacari and I have spoken many times of the gods. What she says grips me deep within, but I cannot accept anything other than the people's way. Since the time of the first Sapan Inca, Manco Capac, when he and his coya rose from the bowels of Lake Titicaca, our people have been blessed with living gods reigning over the empire.

Manco Capac was the child of Lord Sun. After he established the reign of his father in Cuzco, the city known as the navel of our world, he left the time of the present to enter the higher world of Hanan Pacha. His son, Sinchi Roca, the child of his full-blood sister queen, then reigned in his place. All Sapan Incas come from the royal bloodline of Manco Capac and their sister queens.

"How can we know Manco Capac was a child of the sun," Pacari asked one afternoon as we sat on a smooth stone deep in conversation. She looked me straight in the eyes, probing my soul with her questions.

"How can we *not* know," I replied, shrugging my shoulders. I have no answer. There is no evidence, only the stories of men. "It is the people's way," I said, turning my eyes from her penetrating gaze to look at the scenery around us.

We arrived at this place at Coya's insistence Pacari have a break from her continual nursing. She told Pacari she planned to nap and counseled her to take a walk in the sunshine. Pacari found me in my quarters and asked if I would like to walk with her to the drawbridge perched on the other side of the mountain.

Would I like to? Spitting llamas couldn't keep me away.

Two playful mongrels followed us out of the city. They were both of medium size — one a shaggy brown, and the other white with black spots. Their frisky antics entertained us as they nipped and yapped at one another other along the climb.

We traveled the narrow trail that wrapped around the mountain and arrived at the spot where we sat in view of the impressive drawbridge suspended along the face of a sheer cliff. The river roared in the distance at the edge of the rainforest jungle.

"I know it is difficult to think so many people are deceived, Huallpa, but if Manco Capac was a god, why did he not live on, as the sun, as the moon, as the other gods our people worship?"

"When the divine Incas are called home to the mansion of their father, Lord Sun, their bodies remain with us," I said. "We see them at the festivals. They come from their houses and the great temple in Cuzco to join in the celebrations."

"Huallpa, this is the people's way, bringing the mummies of dead Incas and Coyas to feasts and entertainments, but they do not live. They do not eat. At death, they are embalmed and their bowels are removed and sent to the temple of Tampu."

Pacari is convinced of what she speaks. She says Creator God spoke to her in her dreams. That He is the only God, and that He made the earth, the sun, and the moon for all people.

In my mind I understand that natural elements like rivers and mountains do not have spirit life within them. Thunder

God seems to have no power of his own. I never hear him when the sun shines. But perhaps Lord Sun is more powerful and refuses to allow Thunder God to speak in his presence.

It is too much to think of now. Much is happening in the kingdom.

Two days ago another chasqui brought updates from the realm. The sons of Huayna Capac make war with one another. When Huayna Capac was ill, he twice named an heir, but when the priests quickly performed their divinations on the sacrificial llamas, they saw very terrible things.

Huayna Capac died before he could appoint his heir, and the priests named Huascar Sapan Inca. Huascar's half-brother Atahualpa would not accept this appointment, even refusing to pay homage to his father by accompanying his body back from Quito to Cuzco. This was a terrible insult to the great Huayna Capac.

Coya is heavy on my mind. The priests plan to leave Machu Picchu and take Mama Ocllo and her attendants to Vilcabamba, the "Valley of God." I am to accompany them with the llamas bearing some of their furnishings and supplies.

Before leaving Machu Picchu, I will have one more dawn at the Gateway to the Sun. Pacari promised to join me before Lord Sun approaches.

The land of dreams hides from me this night. I lie awake in my quarters in the red stone buildings of the priests, my mind traveling along many paths.

So much has happened since Situa. The hammering of stone has filled my chest with hardness and strength. I have grown taller and darker laboring in the sun. I am not the same person that only a short time ago sat weaving in the allyu with my family.

I am now 14 years — a man ready to begin the next season of life, wondering where tomorrow's path will lead.

Pacari. I cannot think she will walk a path I do not share. She cares for me, I am certain, but we have no parents to arrange a marriage — if she would like to marry. Perhaps we will speak of this in the morning that must surely be arriving after this long night.

I surrendered the battle, unable to gain entrance to the land of sleep hiding from me. Rising from my mat, I rolled it in preparation for the journey ahead. All else was readied the day before.

My eyes adjusted as I stepped into the dim light, bringing steps into focus that led to the Gateway of the Sun on its perch above the city. A chinchilla scurried past, and I chuckled remembering the night Taruca sent me to the rock pile along Hatun Nan. This time I gave way to the fuzzy rodent. I did not want a repeat of the behavior of his relative along the trail, nor to smell of animal urine when I meet lovely Pacari.

I arrived at the Gateway and turned to see the magnificent city below. Pacari was just beginning her journey up the steep stairway, still a long way off and looking as small as the chinchilla I met earlier. I sat on the grass to wait for her and the coming sunrise.

What will happen to Machu Picchu when we leave? Civil war weakens our nation—a nation already ravaged by sickness. The empire collapses around us, while sturdy Runa buildings stand strong and sure.

Will Huascar or Atahualpa reign? Will they come to this place of refuge and gaze at the stars in its observatories?

I have heard through Pacari that Huayna Capac received a prophecy of strangers who would come and destroy both the empire and the religion of our people. The priests say this can never happen, but is it possible?

Coya. I worry for her. Will she return with the next Sapan Inca? She is old and frail.

Looking out over the mountains, I think of how they came to be. The work of Creator God is more amazing than that of Runa laborers. He made the mountains, yet my people reshape them with their building. Why doesn't Mountain God stop us?

Inti, Lord Sun, never alters his course. He must get angry, yet he never moves to show his anger. And Mama Quilla, Moon Goddess, she is the same. Month after month, year after year, the gods remain on their paths. Do they hear the prayers of the people? Do they receive the sacrifices killed upon their altars or the grain and chicha offerings poured out before them?

Taruca. My little deer. I miss her smile and bright, innocent eyes. Her songs brought joy to all. What if Pacari is right? Did my precious one give her life to a god who will never know it? Why would Inti desire the life of one so sweet? Would he not have more pleasure watching her live?

Creator God gives life. How can priests decide to take that life away? And for what reason?

"Help me," I prayed to Creator God. "Help me to know the truth."

Pacari's face rose above the crest. Light shines in her eyes. She said she knows the path of truth, but do I believe her? Am I willing to walk in it?

Change wrestles our land of abundance, and I am pinned in its grip. This contest differs from the wrestling matches of the boys in our ayllu. From those, we brushed the dust off our clothing and helped each other up.

Pacari and I sat in silence as the sun crept over the mountain, slipping its first shining rays out to wake the royal city below.

Pizarro

CHAPTER 10

Vilcabamba
The Last Stronghold

The passage took several days. Machu Picchu is evacuated, and Queen Mama Ocllo is safe in Vilcabamba. We are with her.

Pacari sleeps beside me. We held hands and exchanged sandals indicating our desire before the priests and the people to act as one. She is now my wife.

With Coya's intervention and blessing, we were able to marry before leaving Machu Picchu. In the haste of leaving the city, the priests did not perform the usual religious rituals, but I believe it was meant to be this way. I seek blessing from no god but One.

I understand now that Creator God provided the earth's treasures for His people. Men should worship Him, and not those things He provided for them. God made the great sun in the heavens. He made the moon for our light at night. He set the stars in their places and fashioned the mountains, rivers, and springs.

The glorious days of Inca rule sets as the sun on the horizon. Rulers supposed to be gods toppled at the hands of bearded men from a land across the great water called Spain.

In the conflict between Huayna Capac's sons, the legitimate Sapan Inca, Huascar, assembled an army of inexperienced men to fight rebelling Atahualpa. Over 25,000 men perished in one terrible battle.

After this military defeat, Huascar again rebuilt his army using peasants from faraway lands. During the next conflict in the capitol city Cuzco, Atahualpa's generals capsized Huascar's golden litter. They captured Huascar, dressing the Sapan Inca in women's clothes and forcing him to eat excrement. He witnessed the executions of his family and attendants before suffering his own violent death. Atahualpa celebrated the victory by drinking from his brother's gold-lined skull.

As Atahualpa prepared to make triumphant entry in Cuzco, the chiefs from the coastal regions warned him the bearded men approached. Walking and riding on the backs of powerful animals, the men entered the countryside from the coast, passing signs of the savage war between the brothers. Mutilated corpses swung from trees, and headless human remains lay in the jungle swamps. The men of the company lost their water as they passed the fearsome sights.

The Runa people had never before seen the muscular animals the bearded men rode upon in such splendor. Ten riders on these animals sent a thousand of our men to flight. The people were in awe. Our llamas only bear the weight of small children and packages. Atahualpa wished to capture these animals for his own use.

Fascinated by the animals and the men's armor and magic sticks that shot out thunder and lightning, Atahualpa formulated a plan. He ordered the city of Cajamarca evacuated, then sent gifts to the invaders. He and his men retired to a nearby bath to execute his scheme.

During this time, the terrified citizens of Cuzco prayed desperately to Viracocha, Creator God. They had witnessed the violent battle in their city and pleaded for deliverance from cruel Atahualpa. Many believed the bearded men were the answer to their prayers, assuming Viracocha sent the invaders to save them. The people began calling the white leader, Francisco Pizarro, by the same name they used to call Creator God, Viracocha.

Pizarro responded to Atahualpa's communication and gifts by sending an interpreter and riders to him where he stayed at the baths near Cajamarca. These men offered assistance to Atahualpa's military and invited him to join them for the afternoon meal the following day. Atahualpa gave the men chicha to drink and welcomed Pizarro's troops to stay in the vacant town plaza of Cajamarca. The stage was set for confrontation.

The plaza of Cajamarca, a great, walled triangle, has only one corner entrance. Pizarro, accepting Atahualpa's offer to use the city, hid troops inside the buildings on the plaza's interior perimeter. Mounted on their large animals inside the buildings with tall entrances, Pizarro's men waited for Atahualpa's arrival.

Atahualpa delayed his coming until after dark, laughing that the bearded men were cowards hiding in fear. He felt safe under the cover of night as he arrived in the plaza with his men.

Carried on a golden litter, Atahualpa entered the city surrounded by hundreds of warriors whooping and shouting words of his power and bravery. In the midst of the arrogant display, a robed holy man from Pizarro's company came forward with a small, black, rectangular object. He opened it before Atahualpa and looked inside on one of the thin sheets with markings, then recited a prayer. He beseeched the Inca to be the friend of his God and His people and invited Atahualpa to speak with Pizarro who waited for him in a nearby building.

The Sapan Inca took the rectangular object and examined it. When he could not open it, and it would not speak its words to him, he threw it to the ground in disgust. The robed man left Atahualpa and delivered the Inca's response to his leader.

When Pizarro learned Atahualpa threw the priest's holy object to the ground, he immediately strode out of the building and entered among the hundreds of Runa warriors. He wore no armor and only four men hurried behind him. Fearlessly, he seized Atahualpa by the arm. A great cry arose from Pizarro's hidden forces as they responded to their leader's boldness and courage.

The bearded men charged the plaza, bursting from the surrounding buildings on their powerful animals. Atahualpa's golden litter tumbled in the panic. Pizarro, still holding Atahualpa's arm, protected the Inca from the falling litter and the attacking soldiers. In the foray, Pizarro sustained an injury to his own hand for his efforts to save the Inca's life.

Runa warriors, petrified by the great animals and thundering sticks, broke down part of the city wall as they scrambled to get away. They climbed on top of one another in a frenzied panic and were slain by the advancing military. In their great fear, none raised a hand to defend himself, and in one day, Pizarro and his men captured Atahualpa and killed six thousand warriors without losing one of their company.

Pizarro returned to his lodging with his captive and ordered native clothing brought to Atahualpa who had been stripped of his royal robes. "Do not take it as an insult that you have been defeated," Pizarro said, attempting to soothe the raging Inca. "We come to conquer this land . . . that all may come to a knowledge of God . . . "[2]

Atahualpa feared the men would kill him, so he offered a ransom in exchange for his freedom. His people labored for two cycles of the moon to fill a large chamber with gold.

But after receiving the gold, the bearded men did not release Atahualpa. They learned from a local man that along with the message to bring the gold, Atahualpa also sent orders to collect troops to march against his captors. During the time the gold was being delivered, troops were assembling under a great captain who made plans to attack Pizarro's camp at night.

Atahualpa was charged with conspiracy and sentenced to death by burning. The defeated Inca protested greatly and begged to be strangled instead to preserve his body for the afterlife. Choosing to accept the bearded men's God to escape this fiery fate, Atahualpa confessed belief in Him. The Inca was washed in a purification ritual, after which he was tied to a post in the square and choked to death. His body remained on display until the next morning when the robed men received it into their temple with much solemnity—a surprising honor bestowed on a cruel and deceitful enemy—an honor such as the Runa people had not seen before.

In one year's time, the two warring brothers, Huascar and Atahualpa, both came to the same end . . . captured by their enemies as their royal litters capsized in battle . . . killed by their conquerors.

Pacari was summonsed by Mama Ocllo's attendant. Coya's health is failing.

Several days passed before she returned to me. She stayed with Coya until her spirit departed Vilcabamba in peace. Priests prepared for the queen's mummy to be housed in Vilcabamba. In days past, her embalmed body would have lead a royal procession into Cuzco, but the bearded men plundered the city and buried the bodies of the previous Incas and Coyas.

The Spanish broke down Inca temples, using their gold and granite to build their own shrines. They defiled the sacred places and destroyed the idols of my people.

Our way of life is forever changed, but I will choose to look for the good and trust Creator God.

CHAPTER 11

Intipunku
The Gateway of the Sun

Memories. So many memories rippled through my mind as the little man in the graying cap disappeared through the Gateway's opening and followed the group of porters down the path. Being in this place and the sight of his snake set off a pulsing flow of pictures and emotions, like a stone striking a pool of smooth water.

Over the past 12 years, the Runa people have suffered much loss. Before the Spanish came, we knew little crime. There was no need of it. Sapan Inca made certain everyone had a job to do and had everything they needed to live. Even children worked, scaring away animals from crops and assisting adults in household duties. In return, the people gave Inca their respect and obedience.

Anyone speaking disrespectfully of Sapan Inca or the gods was thrown from a cliff. Hands, feet or both were cut off those caught stealing. The treatment of criminals was harsh, but it created a safe environment for the people to live.

The government cared for the criminals who survived their severe punishments. Every day, in repayment for their deeds,

91

officials forced criminals in their districts to sit at the city
gates and tell others of their crimes.

When a Runa man left his home, he did not seal his door
to keep people from entering. He placed a stick on it simply
to show he was away. We had no locks or prisons.

Although warriors were fierce, and battles brutal, our day-
to-day existence was relatively peaceful. Even the women
and children offered in sacrifice met their ends willingly,
calmly, for the good of the people.

Our traditional Runa greeting explains the Inca ideal:

"Ama sua, ama kjella, ama lllulla."

"Don't lie, don't cheat, don't be lazy."

The words of the common people were true, our actions
honest, and our ethics admirable.

With the Spanish came disease and crime. Change swept
uninvited across the land. Disreputable men stripped much
of our national treasure for selfish gain. These are undeniably
true and disheartening facts, but with the losses, we must
also acknowledge gains achieved in other areas.

The Spanish have ways to put their words on a material
called paper which they make from trees. They write their
words and read them back again—a great accomplishment.
The Runa people use quipus to record numbers, but the
words are not saved except in the minds of the people and
the storytellers.

Wheels and horses ease our work and transportation
needs. I think of what our architects and masons could have
accomplished with the benefit of these rolling circles and
powerful animals.

Steel tools speed building and farming to a pace we never imagined. We no longer toil from sunrise to sunset, and the shortened work days provide more free time for family and pleasure.

Although the tools and animals lighten the burden of work, most daily tasks did not previously seem hardships when joined with family. However, men now choose their trades and may own the animals and the lands they work. The Sapan Inca's authoritarian rule deprived all but the nobles of these privileges, and the people paid high taxes to provide for the extravagance enjoyed within the palaces and temples.

Farmers kept only one-third of their crops, one-third going to the Inca and one-third offered to the gods. Down to the smallest allyu, government mandated the minutest details of Runa life, such as the clothing and patterns woven and worn.

The Spanish tell the people about Creator God. They use the resources of our land to spread the knowledge of God to people who do not know Him. Though we lived without true understanding of Him, my people believed in His existence, worshipping and praying to Him. They called Him Viracocha, the same name they called the bearded Spaniard Pizarro.

I am saddened when I remember those offered in vain to lifeless idols, especially my own dear Taruca. So much blood spilled out in ignorance, when the Holy Book calls its followers to be *living* sacrifices.

I pray that God has mercy on those who have entered the spirit world not knowing the "holy things" they worshipped were not gods, but divine creation.

After Coya's death, Pacari and I journeyed to my family home and ayllu on the outskirts of Cuzco. Nana was happy to see us — and the fluffy llamas ready for shearing. I returned to weaving textiles, creating again the patterns of my community.

The sound of a tripping rock drew my attention below, and I looked down the steep stairway to see Pacari climbing up the path. Baby Urpi, safely secured in a colorful manta tied about her mother's shoulders, smiled and waved at me. My heavy heart lightened at the sight of my wife and our little girl. Beside her Tupac darted in and out, off and on, in front and behind her on the granite trail. Such a bundle of boyish energy.

Little Taruca trails behind him, chasing after her brother as her namesake once shadowed me.

"Look, Father," Tupac said, pointing to the porter with the snake.

"I see, Son," I said, my mind easing back from the past to focus on my family coming up the side of the mountain.

"Taruca, watch out!" Tupac yelled. "Mac'aqway is coming for you!"

One look from Pacari stopped the playful boy from further teasing. It seems little girls named Taruca are all easily frightened by the snakes on these green mountains.

Thinking again of the snake, I recalled the holy words the monks teach my people from the book of sacred writings. They speak of a metal serpent lifted in the wilderness by a great leader named Moses. This snake was a symbol of the true Son God to come.

The monks teach the people that Creator God did not cross the great water leaving His creation in the care of lesser gods. He watched over the people. He knew they could not enter the spirit world of paradise without a proper covering, like the manta of such importance to my people.

Yes, selfish men plundered our land, but perhaps Creator God did answer the prayers of the people gathered in Cuzco as they cried out to Him for a deliverer. Although the Spanish men were not all noble in the way they treated my people and our land, neither were the Inca rulers they unseated. I have learned that even though a chasqui is a flawed person, the message he carries still holds value. The Message, the revelation of Creator God and His word, carried to my people by the Spanish is valid, even when delivered by men who succumbed to gold's temptations of power and riches.

At the feast of Situa celebrated in my thirteenth year, I heard Pachacutec's prayer. The Inca said, "so the people do not suffer and, not suffering, believe in you." I know now that Creator God is real—not only in the good days of feasting and provision, but also in times of struggle and need.

Some of my people resist the ways introduced by the Spanish, but numerous more accept the changes. It is the Runa way to take each day for what it has to offer.

The word Inca means "children of the sun." Standing in Intipunku, the Gateway of the Sun with my family, I am filled with wonder. Creator God did have a Son—not a glowing circle tracing an unchanging course in the sky—but He came Himself as a man God who walked the same earth He created.

All who believe in Him gain entrance through the gateway of the Son Jesus to eternal life in the spirit world.

I believe. I will listen to His Words and follow His honorable teachings. I will share with my people who have not yet heard the true Gateway of the Son.

EPILOGUE

The people now known as Incas called themselves "Runa" meaning "the people." They were later identified by the name of their god, a man called Inca who professed to be deity. The first Inca, Manco Capac, claimed to have risen with his sister bride from a lake in the Andes Mountain region. The ruse fooled the superstitious Indians and began the 96-year reign of the mighty Inca Empire.

Our story started in 1524, at the beginning of the demise of the Empire. Ravaged by small pox, half the Runa population died of the disease by 1527.

Prior to their arrival on the South American shore, Spanish conquistadors received orders from the pope to convert the pagan Indians. This mission thrust Francisco Pizarro to fame as he led a band of less than 200 men to defeat the millions of people controlled by the mighty Inca Empire.

Vilcabamba was the last free Runa city and the final outpost of the people attempting to evade advancing Spanish military. In 1567, Titu Cusi, a member of the Incan royal bloodline, declared allegiance to the king of Spain swearing to keep the peace and placing himself "of his own free will . . . under the power and strength of the Kings of Spain."

Although Huallpa is a fictional character, a man like him may well have lived to see the changes that took place within the 43-year span before Pizarro's arrival and through the time of the Empire's final surrender to the Spanish crown.

On a side note, Pizarro was killed by a Spanish conquistador in a conflict for control of Cuzco in 1541.

Decapitated, his head and body are encased in separate wooden boxes inside a glass coffin on display in a cathedral in Peru's new capitol city Lima.

The road called Hatun Nan by the Indians is now known as the famous Inca Trail. Each year, thousands of tourists hike the trail from Cuzco to Machu Picchu, the same path Huallpa and Taruca traveled on their journey.

The Runa people were highly intelligent and innovative. They were the first known to cultivate potatoes, popcorn and chocolate. They were also the first to tame and herd llamas. As documented, their architectural achievements were astounding.

The people performed successful brain surgeries using cocaine derived from the coca plant to make anesthetics. Peruvians still drink tea made from the leaves of the coca plant, which does not carry the narcotic effect of the stimulant drug. It did, however, take this author's headache away when traveling in the area.

Discussion Questions

How do the parenting practices of the Runa people differ with current philosophy? Cite some strengths and weaknesses of both cultures.

Religious celebrations are integral to most faiths and cultures. Did you find any similarities between the Inca rites and your own faith? What did you find unusual or different?

Huallpa received advice from the priest to travel with more experienced men. In what ways did he and Taruca benefit from heeding the priest's counsel?

The intelligence and expertise of Inca architects and craftsmen were phenomenal. How do you think they knew to build the complex, towering structures still standing today?

How does your life differ living in a democratic country from the Runa people who lived under authoritarian Inca rule? In what ways was it better/worse then? In what ways is it better/worse now?

Child sacrifice is something we can barely grasp in today's society. Why do you think people were willing to sacrifice their children?

Pacari claimed to gain her revelation of the One God in a dream. Do you think people can be lead in right paths by their dreams? Why or why not?

What was the most interesting cultural practice you learned about the Inca people through this book? About the Spanish conquerors?

Considering Incas married full-blood sisters, the mental health of the offspring most likely deteriorated through the generations. Did any of the Incas' behaviors lead you to believe their reasoning might have been impaired?

How did religious beliefs influence the lives of the Runa people and the Spanish?

Do you think the Spanish were wrong to execute Atahuallpa after they discovered his deception and the surprise attack he was planning?

Without supporting or condemning the means they used, do you think the Spanish were wrong to attempt to bring their faith to the Runa people? Why or why not?

Glossary

Amaru – a type of large snake.

Amulet - a small object worn to ward off evil, harm, or illness or to bring good fortune; protecting charm.

Atahualpa – (1502-1533) the 13th and last sovereign emperor of the Inca Empire, son of Huayna Capac, brother of Huascar

Ayllu – a clan or kinship group of related families who lived close together. They usually worked together and shared their crops and livestock.

Cacao - a small tree native to South America that produces fruit year-round commonly used to make cocoa.

Capacocha – child sacrifice, the ritualistic killing of children in religious practices.

Chasqui – agile and highly-trained runners that delivered messages, royal delicacies and other objects throughout the Inca Empire, principally in the service of the Sapan Inca.

Chicha – a fermented drink, wine or beer made from maize.

Chinchilla – a small rodent native to South America with dense, soft, silvery-gray fur.

Chuchau – a plant similar to aloe, native to South America (one of the porters).

Chuno – potatoes dried in the sun and crushed to a powder.

Coca – a plant that grows in the Andes Mountains, the raw material used to manufacture cocaine, chewed and brewed into tea to stave off hunger and control pain.

Condor – one of the largest flying birds in the Western Hemisphere, part of the vulture family with black feathers and up to a 10-foot wingspan.

Coraquenque – a rare and curious bird found in the desert country among the mountains, reserved for the exclusive use of supplying feathers for the royal headgear of the Inca.

Coya – queen, the full-blood sister of the Inca.

Cusi – Joy, pleasure, or content (Taruca's favorite llama).

Cusichaca – a bridge on the Inca Trail.

Cuzco – the capital city of the Inca Empire.

Gateway to the Sun (Intipunku) – the gateway from Machu Picchu to the Inca Trail leading to the capital city Cuzco, a stone structure created on the mountain pass which created a laser-like shaft of light during different seasons that shone in the temple windows.

Guaman – province/political division (cousin to Huallpa).

Hanan Pacha – the future and spirit/higher world, heaven.

Hatun Nan – the road between the capital city of Cuzco and the royal city of Machu Picchu, known popularly as the "Inca Trail."

Hembra – female alpaca or animal

Hitching Post of the Sun (Intihuana) - a huge granite stone with a pillar in the middle of it used for ceremonies and to predict the solstices and the time of year.

Huallpa – Son of joy (the main male character).

Huascar – Inca Huayna Capac's son who fought a bloody civil war with his half-brother Atahualpa for the rule of the kingdom after his father's death.

Huayna Capac – 11th Inca.

Huilca – a tree yielding seeds used to prepare an intoxicating powder that induced a hypnotic state accompanied by visions. Snuffed during ceremonies by priests and Incas.

Inca – the Indian people living during the Incan Empire used this term to describe the Sapan Inca, the emperor; the Spanish later called all the citizens of the realm Inca.

Inchic – peanuts (one of Taruca's female llamas).

Intipunku – see "Gateway to the Sun."

Jakima – simple, ribbon-like beginner weavings.

Litter – a box-like seat used to transport royalty, constructed on poles carried by strong men on each side.

Llama – a domesticated member of the camel family that provides wool and is used to transport goods, able to carry up to about 50 pounds.

Llamera – Quechuan girls who take care of llamas; they are known for making up pretty songs and dances while they pasture the animals in the hillsides.

Llautu – a turban-like headdress made with strips of fringed fabric coiled around the head.

Mac'aqway – snake.

Machu Picchu – commonly known as "The Lost City of the Incas" discovered in 1911 by Yale Professor Hiram Bingham on his quest to locate the last Incan stronghold Vilcabamba; a royal retreat and observatory high in the Andes Mountains.

Mama Ocllo – mother of Inca Huayna Capac.

Mama Quilla – name of the "moon goddess."

Manco Capac – the first Sapan Inca reportedly originating from the bowels of Lake Titicaca with his full-blood sister and queen, divine son of Lord Sun.

Mani – peanut (one of Taruca's female llamas).

Manta – a Peruvian textile woven in two pieces and then sewn together; used to carry things when tied to the shoulders or to sit on.

Micos – a type of monkey (one of the porters).

Muru – smallpox.

Nana – a woman's sister.

Orejones – nobility who had their ears pierced with golden bodkins creating openings for enormous pendants; literally meaning "big ears."

Pacamayo – a valley on the Inca Trail/Hatun Nan.

Pacco – priest.

Pachacutec – ninth Sapan Inca credited with expanding the empire across much of South America.

Pisco – bird.

Puma – a cougar/mountain lion.

Puric – able adult man, head of household.

Qoricancha – the temple of the sun in Cuzco.

Quechua - the Native American language adopted by all captives of the Inca people.

Quinoa – a grain made from a plant that has edible seeds.

Quipu – an accounting tool that uses knots in colored spun and plied threads, some have just a few strands, but some have up to 2,000 strands.

Quito – the capitol of the northern half of the Inca Empire located in modern-day Ecuador.

Runa – what the people under Inca rule called themselves.

Sacsayhuaman – a huge fortress that guarded Cuzco. The name means "satisfied falcon" and it served as a stronghold for the Incas and had huge storehouses and a temple.

Sapan Inca – the ruling Inca.

Sinchi – chief, leader (the head builder in Machu Picchu).

Situa religious purification festival that takes place annually in the capital city Cuzco.

Solstice - The two occasions each year when the position of the sun at a given time of day does not seem to change direction. In the Northern Hemisphere, the summer solstice occurs around June 21 and is the longest day of the year. The sun stops getting higher in the sky, and the days begin to grow shorter. The winter solstice, which occurs around December 21, is the shortest day. The sun stops getting lower in the sky, and the days begin to grow longer.

Tambo – courier post where relay runners stopped for food, water and shelter.

Taruca – deer (Huallpa's sister, also his daughter).

Totora – reeds, rushes (Huallpa's cousin).

Urubamba Valley – called the "Sacred Valley," a flat bottom valley and one of the most productive areas in Peru.

Urpi – dove (Coya's granddaughter and Huallpa's daughter).

Vicuna - a smaller relative of the llama that produces the softest, most delicate wool used in fine clothing.

Vilcabamba – last stronghold of the Incan Empire.

Villa Umu – high priest in Cuzco who married and competed in authority with the Inca.

Viracocha – name the Incas gave to the invisible Creator God who they believed made the lesser gods.

Wayllacha – a dance practiced in big groups in almost every city of the Andes during celebrations.

Yancuna – a class of servants.

Yarqha Haspiy – songs sung while working on water canals, sung by ladies while the men work.

NOTES & RESOURCES

Chapter 2:
[1] Inca poetry translated by John Curl, published in *Ancient American Poets*. Used with the permission of Bilingual Press.

Chapter 10
[2] Quote taken from Pizarro's secretary, Francisco de Xeres, documented in "Capture of an Inca King: Francisco Pizarro."

amulet. (n.d.). *Dictionary.com Unabridged (v 1.1)*. Retrieved March 24, 2007, from Dictionary.com website: http://dictionary.reference.com/browse/amulet

Bingham, Hiram. *Inca Land: Explorations in the Highland of Peru*. www.gutenberg.org. No copyright in U.S. <www.gutenberg.org/etext/10772>.

Cobo, Father Bernabe. *Inca Religion and Customs*. Austin, TX: University of Texas Press, 1990.

Culture Incas – History of the Incas. www.welcomeperutravel.com. February 27, 2007 <www.welcomeperutravel.com/english/the-inkas/history-inca.html>

Curl, John. *Ancient American Poets*. Tempe: Bilingual Press, 2005.

Frazer, James George, Sir. *The Golden Bough.* New York: Macmillan, 1922; Bartleby.com, 2000. <www.bartleby.com/196/>. Feb. 20, 2007.

Getz, David. *Frozen* Girl. New York: Henry Holt and Company, Inc., 1998.

Harris, Eric R. *The Costume of the Inca.* www.hartford-hwp.com. February 28, 2007 <www.hartford-hwp.com/archives/41/414.html>

Hunefeldt, Christine. *A Brief Hisory of Peru.* New York: Lexington Associates, 2004.

Incan Empire. www.encyclopedian.com. February 19, 2007 <www.encyclopedian.com/in/Incan-Empire.html>

"Incan Names." www.lowchensaustralia.com. February 19, 2007 <http://www.lowchensaustralia.com/names/incanames.htm>

Malpass, Michael A., *Daily Life in the Inca Empire.* Westport, CT: Greenwood Press, 1996.

Marrin, Albert. *Inca and Spaniard: Pizzare and the Conquest of Peru.* New York: Atheneum, 1989.

Pizarro, Francisco. *Capture of an Inca King.* www.fll.vt.edu. March 26, 2007 <www.fll.vt.edu/Culture-Civ/Spanish/texts/spainlatinamerica/pizarro.html>

Prescott, William Hickling. *The History of the Conquest of Peru*. www.gutenberg.org. February 20, 2007 <http://www.gutenberg.org/etext/1209>

"Quechua Dances." www.andes.org. February 19, 2007 <http://www.andes.org/dances.html>

Secrets of Lost Empires" Inca. DVD. Nova. 1997.

Solstice. *The American Heritage® New Dictionary of Cultural Literacy*. February 22, 2007 <http://dictionary.reference.com/browse/solstice>

"The Inca's Civilization and Language." www.incashomestead.com. February 19, 2007 <http://www.incas.homestead.com/inca_language_quechua.html>

"The Mystery of Inca Child Sacrifice." www.exn.ca. February 25, 2007 <http://www.exn.ca/mummies/story.asp?id=1999041452>

Time Life's Lost Civilizations: The Maya – The Inca. DVD. Time Life Video. 2002.

About the Author

Lori Wagner is a gifted author, communicator and teacher whose passion and energetic spirit delight readers across the nation. In 2006, Lori established Affirming Faith as a vehicle to provide quality educational, inspirational and fictional resources to readers of all ages. She and her husband Bill live in Rochester Hills, Michigan, with their children where Lori is active in her church and community.

For information on bulk orders of
Gateway of the Sun, or to
schedule Lori Wagner for a
speaking engagement, contact:

Affirming Faith
1181 Whispering Knoll Lane
Rochester Hills, MI 48306
(248) 909-5735
loriwagner@affirmingfaith.com
www.affirmingfaith.com